THE
IMPACT
of
YOU

Kendall Ryan is the *New York Times* and *USA Today* bestselling author of contemporary romance novels, including *Hard to Love, Unravel Me, Resisting Her* and the *Filthy Beautiful Lies* series.

She's a sassy, yet polite Midwestern girl with a deep love of books, and a slight addiction to lipgloss. She lives in Minneapolis with her adorable husband and two baby sons, and enjoys cooking, hiking, being active, and reading. Find out more at www.kendallryanbooks.com

THE
IMPACT
of
YOU

Kendall Ryan

HARPER

Harper
An imprint of HarperCollins*Publishers*
1 London Bridge Street
London SE1 9FG

www.harpercollins.co.uk

A Paperback Original 2015
1

Copyright © Kendall Ryan 2013

Kendall Ryan asserts the moral right to
be identified as the author of this work

A catalogue record for this book
is available from the British Library

ISBN: 978-0-00-813408-2

Set in Minion by Born Group using Atomik ePublisher from Easypress

MIX
Paper from
responsible sources

FSC
www.fsc.org   **FSC** C007454

FSC is a non-profit international organisation established
to promote the responsible management of the world's forests.
Products carrying the FSC label are independently certified
to assure consumers that they come from forests that are managed
to meet the social, economic and ecological needs
of present and future generations.

Find out more about HarperCollins and the environment at
www.harpercollins.co.uk/green

Chapter 1

Avery

Thirty minutes into my first college party, and I'm ready to smack someone in the face with a shovel. My first problem is that I'm wearing the most ridiculous shade of pink. Madison's doing, of course. Tugging at the hem of my hideous shirt, I plaster a fake smile on my face and try to act as if I own this new look.

Compared to Madison in her tight jeans, low-cut black top, and sexy three-inch heels, I look *cute* in my pink outfit. And I hate that word. Cute is what you use to describe a teddy bear or a three-year-old, and it only demonstrates that I don't belong at this frat party filled with gorgeous half-dressed girls grinding on the dance floor. *Fuck my life.*

Sighing, I push a chunk of hair behind my shoulder and take another sip of the now warm beer in my hand. Madison thrusts her arm around my waist, bumping her hip against mine in time with the music. I smile at her attempt.

'Need more to drink?' she asks above hip-hop music so loud I can feel the beat vibrating in my chest.

I look into my still full red plastic cup. 'I'm good.' I hate the taste of beer, but manage to take another sip. Tonight is all about blending in. And something tells me being the stone-sober girl with a perma-frown etched into her face isn't the way to do it.

Madison and Noah are convinced this will be my year. They have grand visions of me loose and carefree, thriving in the college social scene despite the contrary evidence I'd presented them as a freshman last year. When they'd dressed me in this pink top earlier – which Noah claimed was actually *rosy coral* – they'd declared me a ripe peach, ready for the picking. I'd barely kept the scowl off my face at the euphemism.

'Mancandy, two o'clock,' Madison announces over the music.

I take my time, subtly turning in the direction she indicates. A group of three guys stands talking near the DJ and, honestly, they're all cute. Either that or my mind won't let me distinguish individual features since my body has no plans of getting involved with anyone. Ever.

'Which one?' I ask, playing along with Madison so I don't disappoint her yet again. I know I make a terrible wing-woman. Noah fills the role a heck of a lot better than me. A fact he's super proud of.

Madison glances at the group of preppy college boys. 'The pretty one.'

Pretty?

Noah steals a glance at the group of guys too. 'Damn, that boy is fucking delish.' He shakes his head.

'Major player, though.' Madison rolls her eyes.

'The pretty ones always are,' Noah adds.

I can't resist looking again for this so-called pretty boy, and when I do, icy blue eyes meet mine and he zeroes in on me with a smirk. His lingering gaze rakes boldly over my body, and I feel the nervous lurch of my stomach. The sights and sounds of the room fade away. Yeah, he's pretty. That's the only way to describe him. He's roughly six-feet tall and lean, but with a hint of muscle. His hair is a warm mix of brown and blond, and his eyes are such a striking blue, it shouldn't have been possible without colored contact lenses. Not to mention the ridiculously long eyelashes that I'd happily murder him for in his sleep.

A warm tingle creeps up my chest. It's a decidedly unwelcome feeling and I swallow a large gulp of beer hoping to extinguish whatever the hell that sensation was. I want to look away, but I can't. He has on dark jeans that fit his lean frame perfectly – slouching a bit on his hips but held in place by a worn leather belt. His T-shirt is plain and navy blue. I like that he isn't overdressed for this thing, like some of the other gel-haired, button-up-shirt-wearing guys circling us. His hair is unruly and rumpled like he'd been in a fight with his comb. I have the urge to brush the strands out of his face. Or use it to tug him in to kiss me. *Where did that thought come from?*

Pretty Boy's eyes stay locked on mine. One corner of his full mouth pulls upward. *Crap.* He caught me staring. I can feel my fake smile wavering. As my cheeks heat up, I look down at my feet that are squeezed into Madison's heels. He has to know how gorgeous he is. Guys like him always do. And he is firmly in male-model territory, so he can't fault me for looking.

'C'mon, Avery, dance with us. You're being a downer,' Madison whines. When I blow her off a second time, she gives up and drags Noah to the center of the living room. She sways and grinds to the beat, obviously hoping Pretty Boy will notice. They gesture for me to join them, but as much as I love them both, this is so not my scene. Noah and Madison are both theater majors, so to say they are dramatic is an understatement. Sometimes I wonder if I cling to them because their flamboyant personalities mask my non-existent one. I watch them shimmy and shake for a few minutes before sneaking another glance at Pretty Boy in the corner.

He's still watching me, so I give him my best attempt at a smile. I'm pretty good at hiding that I'm wounded, that my life blew up in a spectacular scandal my senior year, and that I still walk around fearful what happened that night will be uncovered. I hold the I-could-care-less-smile in place. I'm just a regular college sophomore in a hideous pink shirt. Move along folks. Nothing to see here.

My cheeks still burn and my heart pounds in time with the music. *It's too damn hot in here.* Too hot to be wearing jeans and a three-quarter sleeve top. Pushing a damp tendril of hair from my face, I pull a breath into my lungs. It only confirms what my body already knows. Even with the show going on in front of him, Pretty Boy is still closely watching me.

The way his eyes lock on mine from across the room holds the promise of something much more intimate than two random partygoers. His deep blue gaze penetrates me and eats away at the calm, cool demeanor I fight to maintain. He looks at me like he knows me all too well, like he sees I'm an imposter. Maybe it's because he's hiding something too. His friends laugh around him while he looks on, bored and unimpressed. I snap my gaze away.

Guys like him bug me for numerous reasons. I hate his overconfidence and the way he's completely ignoring the girl grinding up on him. Like he couldn't be bothered to pay attention to anyone he deems unworthy of his affections. *Cocky bastard.* If he doesn't want her he should send her on her way, put her out of her misery. Blond bimbo or not, she's still a person.

Watching the poor girl conjures up memories I can't deal with. I hate that I was once that girl. Pretty Boy continues to rake his gaze over every inch of me. Well, if this jerk thinks I'm an easy conquest, he's sadly mistaken. Lifting my chin, I avert my gaze and force my smile to remain in place. I throw a glance at Madison and Noah who are full-on impersonating Lady Gaga at this point, and deciding my friends won't miss me, I make my way through the crowd toward the back door. And freedom.

4

Chapter 2

Jase

The blond skims her nails over my chest and lowers herself down until her face is level with my groin. She bites her bottom lip and blinks up at me seductively. Too bad this is doing absolutely fucking nothing for me. I attempt a smile, but my face feels tight and unnatural. I grip her arms and haul her up, bending to whisper near her ear. 'Sorry, baby. Not tonight.' Disappointment crosses her features, but she nods, and walks away.

A year ago this would have been my favorite way to spend a Saturday night. Girls? *Check*. Drinking? *Check*. Raging party with my friends? *Double Check*. Not so much anymore. I don't miss drinking too much and waking up next to someone I can't remember.

But the main reason this holds no appeal? I was plastered the night I got *the call* from my dad last semester. I had to wait until morning before attempting the three-hour drive home to see my mom, all pale and gray in that hospital bed. After spending a tortured night, shattered without any way to fix it, drinking becomes a far less important priority.

My best friend Trey leans over. 'Damn man, you don't even have to try. It's like you set off some radar that attracts them. Come. Fuck. Me,' he says in a robotic voice.

I shove his shoulder. 'Shut up, you know it's not my fault.'

'No, the superior genetics bred into you by the Congressman and the MILF ensure you get ass easily and often.' He shakes his head. 'Fucking lucky bastard.'

I chuckle, brushing off his comment. The truth is I didn't ask for the attention, and I rarely sleep around anymore. But I'd earned my reputation during my freshman and sophomore years banging pretty much every girl in sight. And now I don't do much to dispel the rumors. It's nice, though, not be on the outs with one guy or another in the house because of whose girlfriend or sister I'd slept with. I'm actually enjoying the reprieve.

I look up and spot a pretty dark-haired girl in the corner. She isn't dressed like the other girls here – her tits and ass aren't on display—and strangely it makes her even more attractive. Her eyes widen and she forces a smile. It's obvious this isn't her scene.

I take comfort knowing I'm not the only one faking it tonight. She's not the type of girl the old me would've bothered with. Meaning her panties aren't ready to drop to her knees at my command. But somehow that only makes me more interested. She tugs at the hem of her pink shirt, looking ready to flee.

'Just wanted to warn you…Stacia's here and was looking for you earlier,' Trey says.

Shit fuck. 'Just what I wanted to deal with tonight. Drunk Stacia.' Sloppy Stacia, crying Stacia, horny Stacia, take your pick. She's usually at least one, if not all of the above.

'You guys broken up again?'

'For good this time.'

He raises his glass in a mock salute. 'Stay strong, man.'

I plan to. We've broken up and gotten back to together so many times, I don't know which way is up with that girl. We dated for a year. Why? I couldn't tell you. I never liked her personality, but I did like her body. Still do, if I'm being honest. And she always shared that with me freely. But hanging out, listening to her talk about inconsequential bullshit… gah, even the sound of her voice frays my nerves.

I glance around the room, looking for the pretty dark-haired girl again. Not spotting her, I lean back against the wall so I can see into the kitchen. People fill pretty much every square inch of the kitchen, living and dining rooms – the only rooms we keep unlocked during parties. And the line for the bathroom is too long, so she couldn't have gone in there. Considering her friends are still dancing in the center of the living room, spilling beer onto our already disgusting carpeting, I know she's not far. That girl looks far too innocent to be wandering around a frat house alone. *Damn.* I hand Trey my beer and go off in search of her.

I step onto the back deck, and it's so dark out, I don't see her at first. The moon is just a sliver and she's facing away from me, sitting on the bottom step. Reddish-brown hair cascades over her shoulders, falling nearly to her waist and blending in against the dark sky. Her back stiffens at the sound of the music flooding the peaceful night. I close the sliding glass door behind me, muting the noise but not blocking it out completely.

The T.I. song playing inside is about giving her whatever she'd like. A testament I currently share, looking at this pretty little thing in front of me.

She turns and catches my eyes. Her expression isn't the reaction I'm expecting. She seems mildly annoyed…bothered by my presence. It's not the usual effect I have on females.

'You shouldn't be out here alone.' I take a step closer.

'Why, are you planning on trying something? Because I can scream really loud.'

The old me would've made some comment about getting her sexy ass in my bed to see exactly how loud I could make her scream, but somehow I know she's not looking for me to be that guy. It's refreshing. I move closer to her into the cool night air, relieved that I don't have to put on the smooth guy act.

'Can I join you?' I ask.

She eyes me carefully, her gaze lingering a moment too long. For a second I wonder if she's going to say no. I can't remember the last time a girl said no to me. She chews on her lip, trying to read me, then clasps her hands together in her lap. 'You can stay, *if* you behave yourself.'

I chuckle softly. What was she expecting me to do? She either has major trust issues, or she's caught wind of my reputation. 'Do you have mace on you? Maybe a rape whistle tucked under your shirt?'

Her eyes narrow slightly. 'Ha, ha,' she says dryly.

I sink to the bottom step beside her and suddenly question what the hell I'm doing out here with her. This girl is sure as fuck too sweet for me to mess around with. But I know that isn't what I want tonight. If it was, I'd be upstairs in my bedroom with the blond from earlier, and maybe her brunette friend too.

'I'm Jase.' I extend my hand toward her.

She looks at it, but makes no move to give me hers.

'I'll just call you Whistle if you don't tell me your name.'

Her eyes are still blazing on mine as she straightens her shoulders. 'If you're trying to pick me up, save us both the time. My answer's no.'

My shoulders vibrate with a soft laugh. 'Pretty sure of yourself, aren't you, Whistle? I wasn't going to ask you out, but your little speech was cute.'

She fixes her mouth in a tight line. 'My name's Avery.'

I've never met an Avery. The name is pretty, and unique – just like her. Her makeup is natural, subtle compared to the high sheen gloss of the blond's lips from earlier. She's pretty but not overdone.

'I haven't seen you here before.'

'That's because I don't typically come to these things.'

She picks up her cup of beer, but doesn't drink from it. It's like she needs something to do with her hands. I know the feeling. I feel oddly clumsy and unsure around her – not something I'm used to.

I don't need to ask why she doesn't come to frat parties. It's obvious this isn't her scene. 'Do you need another drink?'

She shakes her head. 'Who am I kidding? I'm not going to drink this.' She dumps the contents of the cup into the grass before setting the empty cup beside her.

'Not a fan of beer? I think I could find you something else if you want it…'

'I'm not a fan of drinking, really.' Her voice is soft, like there's some faraway memory pulling at her attention.

Now that I've turned to face her, I can't look away. Her eyes are a mesmerizing shade of green and her hair looks faintly red when it catches the light. She has soft, delicate features, high cheek bones, a full mouth and pretty wide-set eyes. She's lovely.

I drag a hand through my hair and turn away because I can't seem to stop fucking staring at her. *Stop being a creep, Jase.* Instead I look out into the backyard – littered with red plastic cups, beer bottles and cigarettes butts.

'Why not?'

'It makes you do stupid things,' Avery says after several long moments.

I simply nod. She has no idea how close to home that statement hits. Did she do stupid things in her past, or is she basing that on the actions of the people inside?

'Why are you out here?' she asks.

'I needed some air. What about you?'

'The same, I guess.' She attempts a smile, but I can tell she's just as out of practice at it as I am.

9

There's something sad about her eyes, and it makes me want to kick the ass of whoever put that look there. Was it some drunk jerk that hurt her? Maybe that's why she doesn't like alcohol.

'I took last semester off,' I say, trying to keep the conversation going. 'And even though I live in a frat house, I guess I'm not ready for the start of the new semester party.'

She looks over at me. 'You're a Delta Sig?'

I nod, glad that she doesn't ask why I took last semester off.

She looks back out into the yard and releases a deep sigh.

This girl is different, and I'm completely thrown off my game. But I kind of like it. She refuses to drool all over me, and I respect her for that. I hate when girls who know nothing about me act as if we're freaking soul mates. It's such a turn off. But Avery seems different. I want to know her.

Avery

Jase remains silent beside me, and I can sense there's something more on his mind than just escaping the party inside – only I have no idea what it is, or why he's chosen me as company. I grin to myself thinking Madison will be proud that I'm out here talking to the Pretty Boy. And pretty, he is. It's almost too much to handle having him this close and personal. He smells freakin' incredible too, like a hint of spicy cologne and a trace of laundry detergent. I want to bury my nose in his neck and inhale, get closer to that delicious scent. Of course I do no such thing.

'What's the most interesting thing about you?' he asks suddenly.

I am *so* not telling him that. His question is an odd one, but I go with it. 'I was adopted.'

'Really?' His gaze flicks to mine.

Whenever I tell people, their eyes light up in wonder, like I'm suddenly special, different. I don't know if they expect me to be from some cool foreign country, or maybe have celebrities as parents, but the truth is nothing like that. 'Not from anywhere interesting. Just Colorado.'

'That's cool. Have you ever been back to visit?'

'Nope. My dads wanted to take me there as a graduation present, but I don't know…' I shrug. 'I'd convinced them I didn't want to go. I actually did. Desperately. But I felt guilty for wanting to. They got uncomfortable whenever I brought up anything about my birthmom, as if they thought they weren't enough for me,' I finish. I have no idea why I'm unloading all this on a guy I just met. It seems Pretty Boy possesses the rare ability to coax the truth from me. Not good.

To his credit though, Jase doesn't react at all to the two dads thing. He just nods and continues picking at the fraying string on his jeans, like he's listening thoughtfully, both to the things I'm saying and what I'm not saying.

The truth is I'd never met my birthmom, but I'd always wanted to. Depending on the mood I was in, I would picture my mom as an elegant model, or during the tougher times of dealing with my adoption, as a homeless bag-lady.

My first impression of Pretty Boy Jase when I watched him inside with the blond was that he was your typical party-loving frat boy. Now, watching him silently pick at the hem of his jeans, I'm not so sure. He seems more comfortable sitting out here in the dark than being inside with his friends.

'So, what's the most interesting thing about you?' I ask, returning his strange question. He chuckles softly, the timbre of his deep voice rolling over me like a seductive wave. 'Hmm.' He considers my question for a moment, looking up at the sky. 'I don't know. But I kind of want to find out, you know?'

I nod. What a pair we make sitting out here alone in the dark. I'm running from my past, and he's trying to discover his future. Either way, it seems we're both over the idea of pointless partying.

As the bash rages on inside, I find solace in the knowledge that I'm not alone.

Jase

I need to direct the attention back to her before I say something stupid. And the way her bright green eyes gaze into mine, who knows what I could admit to if pushed. 'So why are you really out here hiding?'

Her eyes flick nervously to mine, like I've uncovered some big secret. Only I have no clue what it is. Avery straightens her shoulders and lets out a sigh. 'I'm not hiding. I just needed a break.'

She acts like being at a party is work, but I can't argue. I'd rather be out here with her too. For a moment she watches me from the corner of her eye. Rather than stare at her like I want to, I continue picking at the blade of grass I've pulled from the ground.

'Why are you bored with life?' she asks.

She has no way of knowing the truth behind her words. Before I can respond, the door opens behind us, blasting us with an unwelcome wave of music. Avery and I both turn to see who's interrupted our hideout.

It's Trey. *Shit fuck.* He staggers toward us, his eyes dancing between me and Avery with interest. 'Stacia's looking for you,' he announces.

I cringe as Avery's eyebrows raise, no doubt wondering who Stacia is.

'I'm busy right now.'

Trey continues, 'Come back inside, man. I need you to divert some of the pussy you attract over to me.' He takes a deep chug from his cup. 'Hell, I'll even take your leftovers.' His eyes dart to Avery's. 'And considering this one's still talking to you, I'm guessing you haven't fucked her yet.'

Avery cringes at his words, and in two seconds flat I'm on my feet.

Avery

Jase stands suddenly and shoves a hand against his friend's shoulder, hard enough to knock him back several steps. 'Go back inside, Trey. Drunk ass,' he mutters to himself.

Trey drags himself back inside, but his visit is a wake-up call. I really shouldn't be sitting alone in the dark with a guy I don't know. A guy who, according to his friend, definitely knows his way around a vagina. That's the last thing I need. When I stand, I see disappointment cross Jase's features.

'I'm gonna go,' I say.

He nods and watches me leave, his hands fisted tightly at his sides.

Back inside, the heat and music are too much. I find Madison and Noah where I left them in the living room, still dancing, only drunker than before. I tug on Madison's arm. 'Hey!' I shout over the music. 'I'm ready to go.'

She stops dancing to frown at me, but doesn't argue. 'Okay.' She grabs Noah's hand. 'Noah-baby, come on!'

He grins, as easy going as ever, and follows us to the front door. I steal one last glance behind me and spot Jase situated on the couch, a different blond perched in his lap, his hands by his sides, doing nothing to stop the lap dance. His expression is bored, and when his eyes find mine, he frowns.

'Let's go.' I tug Madison, more forcefully this time, and we head out the night. I hate the feeling of Jase's eyes on my back as I retreat. I hate that I thought we shared something outside.

When we reach the dorm, Noah follows Madison and me into our room, which has become a common occurrence. He hates his roommate this year. Apparently he was paired with some gay-bashing jock. Which sucks. Madison and I have told him to go to housing services and try to get switched. But each time he just shrugs. I kick off my shoes and fall onto my narrow twin bed. I'm ready to crash, not used to staying up so late, but apparently Madison and Noah are still in the dancing spirit. Madison turns up the music and they begin rehearsing the dance they've choreographed for *Call Me Maybe*. Even though I've seen it a million times, when Noah steps forward and sashays across our tiny room, it still makes me laugh. God, I love these two. It's times like this I wonder, why can't I just hide in my bubble? I have the two best friends a girl could want.

What's so wrong with being the careful sophomore who's best known for turning in her homework early? Or the girl who's always around on weekends to let streams of drunk kids back into the dorms at night because she has nothing better to do? Oh God, yeah, that was bad. But the question is… do I want to change my reputation? I've worked hard to earn it – to stay under the radar. And I know if I jump onboard with the Madison school of crazy, all that would disappear.

I've achieved the anonymity I crave– so why do I feel so restless?

It's why I choose this middle-of-nowhere-Iowa private college – because practically no one from my high school was coming here, which made it all the more appealing. Safe. Even though my dads wanted me to follow in their footsteps, go to State and become a Viking, I convinced them that this was what I wanted. Now I'm not so sure.

I replay my conversation with Jase over in my mind. What was it about him that felt so familiar?

Madison prances over to me, lip syncing with gusto. '*Here's my number, call me maybe.*'

My mouth curls into its usual crooked grin, watching them sing their hearts out. Once the song is over, Madison removes her bra from under her shirt and thrusts off her jeans. She has zero modesty – in front of me, Noah, or anyone really.

Madison is my opposite in every way. I wear my hair loose like a curtain to hide behind –the longer, the better. Madison's is cropped close to her shoulders in a sleek bob that she threatens to chop on a regular basis. She's also blessed with a flawless olive complexion, while I'm pale except for the fine dusting of freckles across the bridge of my nose and top of my chest. Speaking of chests, hers fits politely inside her shirt, two nicely rounded lady bumps. Mine? Not so much. My boobs and I have never gotten along. Mine spill over a C, but I refuse to buy a bigger size, so I've taken to wearing sports bras exclusively since last year. Though it's not because I care for jogging. They're just more manageable this way. Of course Madison had a field day with that information, outraged that I'd taken to keeping my lady parts strapped down. She even tried to get Noah involved in making a case to free my boobage, to which he replied, 'Eh. I could take 'em or leave 'em. But I have heard guys like those things.' We all cracked up laughing, and that was pretty much the end of that conversation.

Madison flops down onto my bed, forcing me to scoot over. Noah stretches out on our futon, where he's regularly been sleeping.

'Did you have fun tonight, Avery?' Madison asks.

I nod. 'Yeah. It wasn't bad.'

She chuckles. 'If there's no one who interested you at that party tonight, you've got bigger issues than I can help you with.'

'There was someone,' I admit, my voice tiny.

'Who?'

'His name was Jase.'

'Jase Owens?'

I nod sheepishly.

Her eyes fly to Noah's, which are just as wide and concerned. 'Oh honey,' he frowns.

'What?' I ask, keeping my voice level.

Madison rolls her eyes and lets out a huff. 'Noah.' She motions for him to explain, anchoring a hand on her hip. Uh-oh, this isn't good.

'How do I put this….' He taps his index finger against his chin, his expression grim. 'He's a shark, babe. You need a guppie.'

I frown. Was Jase a shark like they thought? After talking with him on the deck, I didn't think so. But then I remembered the large-chested girl who planted herself in his lap just minutes later. Her breasts weren't bigger than mine, but she had no problem putting them out there in people's faces. And Jase did nothing to remove her from his personal space.

Madison pats the top of his head. 'Well said, tootsie roll.'

'Relax guys, it's not like I'm gonna do anything about it.'

Madison's eyebrows dart up. 'Baby, you wouldn't even know what to do with a guy anyway.'

I don't argue. I don't tell her she's wrong. It doesn't matter because it's not like I'm planning on getting involved with anyone. Especially Jase. Getting close to people means running the risk of exposing my past. And that is not okay with me. Not even Madison and Noah know, God love 'em.

'Night guys.' I flick off my lamp, plunging us into darkness and curl onto my side, letting the numb feeling overtake me. I can't believe I'd opened up to Jase tonight – thinking we'd shared some sort of moment, telling him about my adoption. That was dumb. No sense in getting my hopes up about Jase, I was safer alone anyway.

Chapter 3

Jase

I hadn't expected to see Avery again, which is why the flash of auburn hair leaves me momentarily stunned. Seeing her in the daylight, I realize she's even prettier than I first realized. But as quickly as I spot her, she's gone – diving for cover behind a dumpster. 'Avery?' I round the corner and see her couched down, knees drawn up to her chest.

Her eyes dart up and meet mine and she lets out a soft groan. She doesn't say anything, just remains hunkered down next to the dumpster. I hold out my hand, offering to help.

Her gaze lifts from mine, searching for something in the distance before she takes my hand.

'Why are you hiding?'

'I wasn't,' she says quickly.

I lift one eyebrow. I can feel her hand trembling in mine.

'Can you just get me out of here?' Her voice has a raspy, pleading quality to it that I can't refuse.

'Where do you want to go?'

Her gaze darts behind me. 'Anywhere but here.'

Sadness flickers in her eyes and instantly I know I'd gladly fuck up whoever had hurt her. 'Come on. If we cut through there,' I point to a trail at the edge of campus, 'my house isn't far.'

She nods, and glances behind her once more before following me.

I have no idea what spooked her, but she's pale and jittery, like she might dart away from me at any second. I'm not sure why, but I can't let her do that. I reluctantly release her hand, but she keeps pace beside me. 'Do you have a class right now?' I ask, needing to break the silence.

She shakes her head. 'I'm done for the day.'

Damn, only eleven in the morning and she's done for the day? I don't take classes that start before noon.

When we reach the Delta Sig house, she hesitates at the front door before stepping inside. It's trashed, as usual.

'This is weird – being in a frat house during the light of day.'

I smile. 'Come on, I'll show you around.'

'How many guys live here?' She follows me through the living room. There's a random dude sleeping on the couch, and Avery looks slightly concerned at this, but continues past him.

'Um, sixteen, I think. The house is just for the juniors and seniors.' We stop in the kitchen and say hi to Drake and Jared. I figure if I introduce her to a few of my roommates – witnesses – she'll be more comfortable following me up to my room. Of course I don't like the way their eyes travel over her sleek jean-clad hips, visually molesting her. 'Come on.' I take her hand again, which has become a natural reaction to her even though I've always hated holding hands, and guide her to the stairs.

She stops cold at the bottom of the stairs, her eyes full of questions. I turn to face her, resisting the urge to brush the strands of hair back from her shoulders. 'I pretty much only hang out in my room. The rest of the house is nasty.'

She smiles crookedly, unable to disagree that my house is disgusting. 'Okay. But no funny business.'

'Right. Unless you initiate it, in which case I make no promises to stop it.'

She swats my arm. 'I won't be starting anything, so don't you worry.'

She follows me upstairs, and I'm glad she can't see the dumb-ass smile planted on my face. She's not at all like other girls I hang out with, and I like that. We climb the three flights of stairs in silence and when I push open the creaky door to the attic, Avery steps around me to peek inside. Taking the unfinished attic meant I had my own room. It didn't matter that I didn't have heat or air conditioning, I had my own space.

I watch as she takes in the queen-sized bed, neatly made in cream and navy bedding, desk and chair in the corner, a tall dresser and my acoustic on a stand in the corner. The room is large and open, with dark plank-wood floors and beamed ceilings. It's freezing in the winter and stifling hot in the summer, but its September, so for the time being, it's perfect. 'What do you think?'

She wanders over to my desk and looks at the corkboard above it where I've tacked various photos, quotes, and clips from magazines. There's a photo from last summer of me and my mom at the beach – before she went cuckoo for Cocoa-Puffs – and another of Trey and me having an impromptu jam session.

Avery points to the one of my mom. 'You look like her. Same eyelashes.'

'I know.' Everyone always freaks over my eyelashes for some damn reason. It's embarrassing.

Then she turns to survey the rest of my room. 'You make your bed?'

I nod. 'Habit I guess. I had to every day growing up. It was the one chore I had to do, and my mom would freak if I didn't.'

She bites her lip, trying not to smile.

'Come sit down.' I slide her backpack from her shoulders and set it on the floor. She sits on the edge of my bed, while I pull out the desk chair for myself. 'So, are you going to tell me what you were hiding from?'

She looks down and the terrified expression on her face is back. *Shit fuck.*

'Hey, I'm sorry. It's okay.' I hold up my hands in surrender. 'You don't have to tell me.'

She swallows, the tension in her shoulders dissipating slightly as she draws a deep breath. 'Thanks.'

'For what?' I pull the chair closer to where she's seated on the bed.

'For being cool with my…crap.' She twists her hands in her lap. 'I guess I expected you to be different. The Jase Owens I've heard about is a major player and always…' She pauses, biting her bottom lip.

'Always what?'

Her cheeks blush the prettiest shade of pink. And on her fair skin, there's no denying her embarrassment. 'Horny,' she finishes.

I crack a slight grin. 'Well that part's true, babe.'

Her eyes widen just slightly.

A sudden knock on my bedroom door interrupts our silence. 'Hey man,' a muffled voice calls through the door. It's Trey. I'm sure he's been briefed that I'm up here with a girl, so there must be a significant reason for him to interrupt.

'Come in.'

His gaze registers Avery perched on the side of my bed like she's ready to bolt, but his eyes slip past her to me. He doesn't recognize her from Saturday night. Not surprising, given he was drunk off his ass.

'Stacia's here,' he says.

Avery's head turns to me, clearly wondering who Stacia is.

'I'm busy.'

Trey chuckles. 'Come out and deal with her pretty ass.'

'Fuck man, tell her I'm with someone.'

'You know she'll just wait. That girl's got no shame.'

Damn. He's right.

'Okay, tell her to come up.'

Chapter 4

Avery

Hiding behind that dumpster seemed important at the time – I couldn't have someone from my past spotting me, so I'd dived for cover. But now, awaiting someone named Stacia, I question what in the hell I'm doing in Jase's bedroom. This isn't me. I don't follow guys home. I certainly don't make myself at home on their beds. This is just asking for trouble. And now clearly he has a girlfriend, which makes me look like an even bigger idiot.

Trey leaves and Jase makes no move to explain. Since it's too late to escape, I wait. A few seconds later, we hear footsteps climbing the stairs to the attic.

A petite girl with long blond hair rounds the corner and her megawatt smile fades as soon as she sees Jase isn't alone.

'Oh. Hey, Jase,' she recovers and leans down to plant a kiss against his cheek.

God, could this be more awkward? I want to die.

Jase, having perfected his bored-with-life look, nods once at her and then flicks his gaze to mine. 'This is Avery. Avery, this is Stacia.'

Stacia turns, but her smile was only reserved for Jase because it fades as she takes me in. There's something she hates about me being up here with Jase, and the inner bitch inside me enjoys that fact. This girl just reeks of fake, and I'm instantly not a fan.

'I didn't know you had someone over.' Stacia's voice goes soft as she turns to Jase.

'Well, I do. Did you need something?' His voice is cool, unemotional.

Damn. This can't be his girlfriend. Otherwise, he's a real asshole. Of course I'm dying to know who she is, but I won't ask. Not sure I could handle hearing that right now. Jase has treated me with nothing but kindness and respect, and I sort of want to continue thinking the best of him.

'No. Just wanted to say hi.' Stacia lifts one shoulder, then drops it and I can't help but notice the way her chest sticks out when she does. The move is practiced, beyond obvious. God, this girl is annoying me in all of thirty seconds. Before the awkward silence has time to fully descend on us, Stacia bounds over toward me. 'You look familiar.'

My heart stops.

Literally ceases to beat in my chest.

I hope to God she has no idea *why* I look familiar. I pull in a breath and shrug, working to convince myself it's just a coincidence. She can't know.

Desperately needing to change the subject, I ask, 'How do you and Jase know each other?'

Jase answers for her. 'Ex-girlfriend.'

Oh.

'Yeah, some days I'm his ex-girlfriend, some days I'm…what am I exactly, Jase, on those nights you call me and beg me to come over?'

'You wish, Stacia.'

She laughs, her mouth curving into a victorious smile. 'Kay, Jase.'

My stomach cramps.

Jase rises from the chair, watching her with guarded eyes, like she's a wild and unpredictable animal.

Stacia laughs again, nervously this time. 'I can see you're trying to impress your new friend, so I'll go.'

His jaw tenses as he bites back whatever he wants to say. He steers Stacia by the elbow toward the door. 'Avery and I need to study.'

Stacia pouts but lets him guide her out into the hall.

Once the door is firmly shut, I look at Jase. 'Are you sure it's okay I'm here?' I ask.

He laughs uneasily and crosses the room toward me. 'You're saving my ass right now. So thank you.'

'How?'

'By helping me get rid of Stacia. She'd hang out all afternoon if I let her.'

I rise from the bed, wondering if he doesn't want company and if I should head out too. 'Oh…did you want me to…'

His firm hands on my shoulders stop me from going any farther. 'I want you to stay.'

The warm weight of his hands is a constant reminder that I'm not as immune to his charms as I'd like. I smile up at him like a lovesick fangirl. *Idiot*. I silently berate myself that I've joined the Jase fan club. 'Okay.'

'Sit. Stay. Get comfortable.'

I sink down to his bed once again, chemistry crackling between us, no matter how much I might want to deny it. 'Okay.'

'I've got psych homework I could do. And you can hide out here, so just relax, alright?'

I want to ask him more about Stacia, but that may lead him to ask why I was hiding, so I zip it and relax on his large queen-sized bed. It's much more plush and comfy than my narrow rock-hard mattress back at the dorms. Mmm. His bed smells like him. It's a scent I instantly decide could be bottled and sold.

Jase turns on soft music and grabs his textbook and a stack of papers from the desk, balancing everything on his lap so he can face me. I grab the book from my early childhood development class and bravely settle back against his mountain of pillows. My eyes dart up to Jase's but he doesn't seem to mind in the least that I've commandeered his bed. In fact, I swear there's a hint of smile tugging his lips.

'So what's your major?' he asks.

'Social work. What about you?' For some reason I expect him to say *undecided*, but he surprises me.

'Psychology. Mostly because it pisses my dad off.'

'What do you mean?'

He grins. 'He's a mayor and wants to make a run for congress. He's always been obsessed with politics…so of course he wanted me to major in political science, or at least business.'

I nod. My dads didn't really care what my major was. And when I told them I wanted to work in the adoption field, they helped me research the social work program.

'It was either that or something artistic, and since I'm shit at art and just okay at music, I figured psychology was a safe bet.'

'Do you at least like your classes?' I ask.

'Yeah, turns out I love it. People are the most interesting thing to me anyway, so it worked out.'

'Did you succeed in pissing off your dad?'

He nods. 'Oh yeah. He blew a gasket.'

We both smile. Why do I get the feeling that Jase is letting me in on things he doesn't normally share? And why do I like it so much? I focus on my book for a few minutes, but reading about attachment disorder is pretty dry, and Jase's mouthwatering goodness is right there on display. It's hard not to sneak glances at him from time to time. A tiny crease marks his brow as he concentrates, and his lips move when he reads – something he makes look both adorable and sexy at the same time.

'So, Stacia's really your ex?'

'Yeah. But she doesn't act like it. And of course my frat brothers give me shit about it all the time.'

It's clear she'd like to take a ride on Jase, ex or not. Hell, maybe she still does, like she implied. I force my eyes back to my book and relax into the inviting bedding. After a few moments of trying my damnedest to read this textbook, I feel Jase's eyes on me again.

'Do you ever think about meeting your…um, the lady that gave birth to you?' he asks, his brows pulled together.

'My birthmom?' I was used to teaching people the correct terminology. He nods.

'Yeah. All the time, actually.'

'So why don't you?'

I shrug. Lots of reasons. I'm not sure how much I should tell him, or how much he really wants to know, but Jase is leaning forward on his elbows, like he's genuinely interested. I don't typically talk about this stuff. But I trust him enough to let him in, which is odd given that I've only known him such a short time and everyone has warned me about him. 'Now that I'm nineteen, I can go and get the records from my adoption without my dads needing to sign off …' I release a slow sigh. It's something I've thought about doing so many times, yet some unknown force holds me back.

'It's not a big deal. I'll figure out what to do eventually,' I add, hoping to lighten the moment.

'Well, let me know if I can help,' he says softly.

'Why would you do that?'

He shrugs. 'Why not?'

I'm genuinely baffled by his interest in helping me. I know I'm not the best company, only Jase doesn't seem to mind. That's probably because he doesn't know much about me. I duck my head at this realization, drawing my chin to my chest. 'You wouldn't like me if you knew more about my past.'

25

He doesn't press for details. He just remains quiet and reaches for my hand. 'I doubt that could be true. And besides, I have waaay more baggage than you, so we're good.'

Yes, but his reputation is out in the open. He isn't hiding behind a curtain, waiting for some horrible big-reveal like I am. Jase is still watching me and his soft expression sends a warm tingling through my chest. I have no idea why it is that Jase Owens – reported manwhore – would have this effect on me. Yet I can't deny that he does. Which is exactly why I'll need to be extra careful around him.

I blink my eyes open to find Jase standing above me. 'Avery, wake up. You fell asleep.' His hand on my shoulder gently rouses me. What? *Noooo.* I shoot up in the bed, stunned and bleary-eyed. I fell asleep? This is so not me. 'I should go.' I leap up from the bed and grab my backpack, hefting it up over one shoulder. 'Do you have class?'

Jase casually looks at his alarm clock. 'My psych class started twenty minutes ago. I didn't want to wake you.'

Oh. 'Jase, don't skip class for me.'

Jase steps closer, closing the distance between us. I have to crane my neck to look up at him, and my pulse spikes at the sudden closeness. 'It's okay.' He straightens the backpack straps, his hand lingering on my shoulders. 'This was more fun.'

What is okay about any of this, I have no idea. His gaze lingers on mine. I should move away, but I won't. 'Can you afford to miss class?'

He lets out a short laugh. 'I'm not dumb, Avery. I had a near perfect grade-point average last semester. And it's only the second week of class. It's fine.'

My surprised expression gives me away.

'What? Not what you expected?'

I turn and flee without another word, needing to use my body for something useful like descending the stairs so I don't do something stupid like lift up on my toes and kiss him like I want to. Once we reach the front door, Jase grabs my backpack, halting my escape.

'Hey, stay out from behind dumpsters, okay?' He brushes the loose strands of hair back from my face, tucking them gently behind my ear.

'I'll try.'

When I get back to the dorm, Madison shoots me a suspicious glare. 'Where were you all afternoon?'

I casually set my backpack on my bed, my mind grasping at a possible explanation. Knowing I'm horrible at thinking on my feet, I break down and admit I was with Jase, making it sound like we casually ran into each other – which we did. And going home with Jase then was just a no-brainer.

When I spotted Marcy Capri earlier, I knew I needed to get out of there before a panic attack took over. She didn't look dangerous, with her frizzy blond hair and faded black yoga pants, but she was. She held a link to my past. She knew the secret that I've worked hard to ensure didn't follow me here, didn't own me. And I know, given the chance, she'd open her fat mouth and blab. It's too juicy a secret not to. I couldn't have that, so I dove behind the nearest obstacle I could find – which happened to be a dumpster. I was shaking when Jase found me.

But Madison doesn't need to know about my dumpster diving adventures. I also fail to mention the nap I'd taken in his bed. That would send her over the edge. No, that little detail will need to remain between him and me, as would the fact that his pillow smelled like a mix of fabric softener and cologne and I could have easily taken it home to enjoy nightly. That detail definitely doesn't need to be shared with anyone. Not Madison and certainly not too-hot-for-his-own-good Jase.

Chapter 5

Jase

I crank up the radio and settle back as the flat highway stretches before me. Having already missed my afternoon class yesterday because of my soiree with Avery, I take off for home, driving three hours just to check on my mom. I never used to bother going home much my first two years away at college. But a suicide attempt changes things. I won't be able to relax or focus on class until I see her with my own eyes.

When I arrive, my dad is immediately in my face, provoking a fight that nearly leads to blows. He treats her like shit, and I've had it with him. But I try to focus on the fact that she seems to be doing better.

It's a quick trip – I take her out to lunch and we just talk. Sometimes I worry she doesn't eat enough, especially when my dad is out of town, which is often. With no one there to cook for, I have a feeling she just doesn't eat. It's more than just taking her out to lunch, though; I need to check on her, to make sure she's okay. I don't know if I'll ever forgive myself for not realizing how close she'd been to checking out. It makes me realize I can't take her for granted.

Settling into the drive home, I should make it back in time for my human sexuality class, the class I've most been looking forward to this semester. Professor Gibbs' infamous lectures have generated plenty of buzz on campus over the years. It should be an easy A, and of course features my favorite topic – sex.

One hand rests on the wheel while the other tugs restlessly through my hair. I can't stop thinking about Avery. Spending time with her yesterday was…unexpected. Her being comfortable enough to fall asleep in my bed? Shocking. And sexy.

I remember her skittish reaction when Stacia said she looked familiar. She looked like she wanted to dive for cover under my bed. Between hiding behind dumpsters to being terrified of my none-too-bright ex, Avery is a mystery. She's like a scared little wisp of a girl I want to coax out of her shell.

Even I'm not sure of my own motivations since I doubt she'll ever be one of my conquests. Which I both like – and don't. She's definitely tempting, with soft curves that fill out her jeans, long unruly hair, and especially her wide green eyes and soft mouth. *Shit.* I'm going to give myself a hard-on if I'm not careful.

I pull into the campus parking lot just as my class is starting. I'm going to be late. Finding the lecture hall a few minutes later, I pause at the doors to look for an empty seat. Professor Gibbs is tall, bald-headed and is pacing the front of the room. The room is full and silent, aside from him. He pauses just briefly as his gaze meets mine, then he returns to lecturing – making a point about society and self-image. I zero in on an empty seat in the back of the room when movement catches my attention. A flash of auburn hair streaks through my vision and makes my heart gallop. *Avery.*

She sits several rows up and her cheeks blossom when she meets my eyes. I can't help but smile at the sight of her. I maneuver between the rows of seats, and a few nasty looks later, I'm in the chair next to her.

'Hey Whistle.'

She rolls her eyes before facing the front once again, but the little curve of her mouth tells me she's happy to see me. That little curve shouldn't make me feel so good.

I lean closer to whisper near her ear. Traces of floral shampoo greet me. 'What'd I miss?'

'I didn't even know you were in this class. You weren't here last week.'

I like that she noticed that. 'I was gone last week – had to check on my mom,' I whisper back.

Her eyebrows draw together and then she turns to the front of the room again. I can't help but notice she already has a full page of notes scrawled neatly across her notebook and is nervously bouncing a chewed, tattered pen in her hand. Abandoning my inspection of Avery for the moment, I tune in to our lecture. Gibbs is a lively speaker, and it's easy to lose yourself in his words. I pull out the syllabus I printed from online and follow along the second week's lesson: You – A Sexual Case Study. Oh yeah, this class is going to be awesome. And Avery's faint blush during the lecture makes it hard to focus.

Professor Gibbs' pacing leads him to the side of the room where Avery and I are seated. He pauses in front of us, pondering his next thought. 'I've structured this class to allow you to explore your sexuality after finding that many of my students received abstinence-only education in high school.' A few people in the room look at each other, wondering where he's going with this lesson, when he continues. 'Abstinence is often not the reality in college, or in high school for that matter. To remedy that, we'll explore gender roles in society like it says on my syllabus, but we won't just pontificate about these topics as obscure things unconnected to who we are. You'll explore your own sexuality through a weekly journaling assignment.'

He passes out stacks of small black notebooks to everyone seated in the front row. The notebooks begin making their way around the room as everyone takes one.

'These are your journals. And to get you started, I'll provide the topic for your first journaling assignment. Turn to the person next to you. Doesn't matter if it's a member of the same or opposite sex.'

I turn to face Avery. Her cheeks were rosy before, but now she's blushing like crazy and he hasn't even given us the assignment. It's so damn cute.

'Open your journal. I want you to check out the person across from you.' A few soft laughs erupt in the room. 'No talking,' Professor Gibbs reminds us.

I remain silent, slouched in my seat, and take in Avery's stiff posture. If this is a study on the other person's comfort level on sex, Avery will win for most uncomfortable. She looks like she's about to flee the room. Why did she even sign up for this class? It's a voluntary elective.

Professor Gibbs explains the journaling assignment. He's looking to make a statement on positive self-image, self-love. Getting young women to see themselves more clearly, accepting, boosting self-confidence, both inside the bedroom and out; and getting young men to take note of more than what's underneath their clothes. My eyes flick to Avery's. She's tuned in to his every word. Even I have to admit, it's an interesting assignment.

The topic of our first journaling exercise is what we find appealing, beautiful about the opposite sex. A few snide comments and laughs circulate the room, until Professor Gibbs redirects us to think about the uncommon body parts, like hands and eyes. Then pushes us to go one step farther. He approaches me and Avery again, stopping in front of our desks. When he asks us each our names, Avery's blush deepens again. He's going to use us as an example in front of the class. I don't care; I just don't want him to embarrass her.

Professor Gibbs turns to Avery. 'You'll partner up and take note of each other's characteristics. For example, Jase's hands…'

He encourages me to lift them for the class to see. I hold them out in front of me awkwardly. 'He would make a good provider with those strong hands.'

Avery's pretty green eyes follow my movements and remain on my hands even after I've lowered them to the desk.

Professor Gibbs returns to the front, leaving Avery and me alone. I don't care that we are in a room full of people. She's fucking turning me on.

Being able to check out Avery for the sake of schoolwork is an amazing thing. She bites her lip and begins jotting something down in her journal. I wish I knew what the hell she was writing. Is it the thing Professor said about my hands? Somehow I doubt it is. Her gaze rakes over my jaw, down my chest, to my biceps, and it's driving me insane. Each look is like a caress. It hits me like a jolt. I can practically feel her undressing me with her eyes. *Shit.* Who is this girl? She's innocent and sexy all at once, and I know I'm in trouble. My heart is pumping fast, and I feel myself getting hard.

I flip open my own journal, needing the distraction. There are so many things I could write about Avery, but staring down at the blank page, I'm unsure where to begin. I've never kept a journal, but I have a feeling writing about her will be easy.

I take a deep breath and try to focus on the non-traditional body parts like Professor Gibbs reminded us. That way I'm not the perv staring at her tits. Which are exceptionally nice, I quickly note. Her head is still tipped down, so hopefully she didn't notice my indiscretion. Damn, she's writing a freaking novel. Is there really that much to say?

I swallow and focus on my notebook, finally writing, *Her soft skin – it makes me want to protect her.* I close the book before she has the chance to see what I wrote. God, I sound like a pussy.

I lean closer to Avery, and she slams her journal closed. But not before I see that she's written an entire page about me. Wow. 'Had a lot to say, huh?' I whisper, offering a weak smile. She makes me feel so unsure and alive all at the same time.

She just shrugs, trying to downplay the assignment. But I can't. There's something happening between us. And I want to explore what it is.

'Do you have class after this?' I ask.

'No. Why?' she whispers back.

'Come get coffee with me.' It's not a question and Avery just nods before turning to face the front of the room again.

The rest of the class drags by, as interesting as the topic is. The soft, feminine scent of Avery distracts me. Once we get outside, I wait for her to come up with an excuse, but she doesn't. She walks by my side, her eyes looking everywhere but at me. And really, that's all the encouragement I need.

Chapter 6

Avery

I watch Jase walk to the counter at the ultra-busy student commons to pick up our coffee order. He leans against the counter, T-shirt stretched across his broad shoulders. I think he's probably flirting with the cashier, or she's flirting with him. Doesn't matter. I'm still mad at myself for how I acted in class. Just because he has many fine features did not mean I had to catalog each and every one in my damn journal. Once I realized he wrote like one line and gave up on the assignment, I felt like a complete idiot.

While I wait for him to return with our coffee, I slide my notebooks from my bag and arrange them on the table, making sure to keep the journal safely in my bag. I don't want Jase snatching it and reading about how I think his eyes are the most mesmerizing shade of blue, like a cloudless summer sky, and being near him makes me feel more alive than I have in a while, makes me want things I thought I never would again.

I can't give my heart away again. Especially considering it hardly still beat inside my chest. Of course, all this is post-Brent. That's often how I think of my life – the me before all the drama of my senior year, and the me after. After I trusted him. After I let myself be used by him. I know I brought it all on myself, but that doesn't erase the past. Looking back, I don't understand how I could have been so stupid.

But when you're in love and desperate for affection, and dealing with the fact you were adopted – it turns out you'll do just about anything for attention. Things I now wish I could take back. But I never can. Even if there weren't witnesses, the act is burned into my memory.

Besides, it's not like Jase is asking for anything from me. Friends, maybe. That I could handle. I think.

I would probably consider dropping the class if Jase weren't in there to witness my defeat. I don't want him to know the subject terrifies me. I want to be brave, open, like the rest of the students seem. I thought taking this class would be good for me, but now I'm not so sure. But one thing is certain – I won't back out now with my tail between my legs. At least part of me wants to see where this will go – especially since it means I'll be seeing Jase every Tuesday and Thursday, all surrounded by the titillating topic of sex. It'll be a wonder if I can survive this semester without spontaneously combusting.

Jase slides into the booth across from me, setting a paper cup of coffee in front of me. 'Cream and a *boatload* of sugar, just like you requested.'

'Thanks.' I try a sip. Jase is still watching me, a lopsided grin across his lips. 'What?'

He chuckles softly, the deep timbre of his voice raking over me, and folds his hands on the table in front of him. 'Fine, I'll do it.'

'Do what?'

He smirks. 'I see no other choice than to become your tutor.'

This time I'm the one laughing. 'You want to be my human sexuality tutor? That's original. And not douchey at all.'

Jase's determined gaze meets mine. 'As tempting as that offer is – and there's so much I could teach you – no. I meant I could tutor you at…life.'

'Gee thanks. Why don't you just admit you think I'm a loser with no life and get on with it.'

'I didn't say loser. Lost…probably. Not having as much fun as you should be…definitely.'

'Rip the Band-Aid off, why don't you.'

Jase settles back against his seat, sliding his cup of coffee toward him in the process. 'Just calling it like I see it, babe.'

He's too relaxed, too smug. I want to lash out and say something to wipe that cocky smile from his face. Instead, I pull a deep breath and reflect on his observation of me. I'm sitting stick-straight in my seat, my stack of textbooks neatly lined up in front of me. And each time Jase has seen me – first at the party, then behind the dumpster – I've been hiding. I wish I could tell him those were isolated incidents, that I'm not really like that, but sadly I am. I realize with a flash of clarity, Jase is right. And suddenly I want more.

I lean toward him on my elbows, weighing his offer. 'So how would this life-coaching work exactly…I'm not saying I'm interested, but if I was…'

'We'd need to begin spending more time together for starters.'

I nod, listening intently. I'm thankful he doesn't know my heart just kicked into overdrive at his words. 'What else?'

Jase abandons his casual posture, leaning in towards me across the table, his brilliant blue eyes piercing mine with intensity. 'I'll issue you challenges as I see fit. You'd have to trust me.'

I fold my arms across my chest. 'I'm not running through campus naked or dropping acid or anything weird like that.'

'I wouldn't ask you to do anything you're not ready for.' His voice is calm and sure.

I can't believe I'm considering this, but I am. 'Why would you want to do all this…I'm not a project.'

'I didn't say you were. Let's just say I could use the distraction right now.'

I know my expression gives me away. I'm beyond confused about what's happening between us and powerless to stop it.

He brushes his index finger over the crease in my forehead. 'Hey, relax.' His voice is just a whisper. 'You're thinking too hard. I'm not going to pry about your past unless you want me to.'

I shake my head, my heart thumping wildly.

Jase's thumb caresses my cheek before he lets his hand fall away. 'You'll let me know if there's someone's ass I should kick, though, right?'

I would giggle at this, if not for the intensity radiating from Jase. 'No. I made my own choices.'

He's silent while he studies me – his blue eyes looking for answers. Answers I can't possibly give him.

'You were young, too trusting, fell for the wrong guy…'

I clear my throat. 'Something like that.'

He reaches for my hand and gives it a squeeze. 'Hey, it's okay.'

I manage a nod, arranging my mouth in a smile. If he knew the truth, he wouldn't be sitting here, being so kind to me. My heart is thudding against my ribcage. 'This tutoring thing…When do we start?'

He glances at his naked wrist. 'Now would be nice.'

I roll my eyes to avoid chuckling at him. 'Fine. What's my first *assignment*?'

Chapter 7

Jase

Avery is unlike any girl I've hung around before. She keeps me in a constant state of curiosity and mild arousal. It's an interesting combination – both my brain and my dick are engaged, which is something new for me. I can easily see this becoming addicting. I want to challenge her to kiss me, but I know she won't. I can't push her that fast. We'll have to work up to that. But I know if she let me touch her, I could own her. Christ, that's a tempting thought. I never felt a possessive spark with Stacia, but something about Avery makes me want to possess her in a way I never have before.

'I'll go easy on you your first time.' I pause, keeping my eyes on hers, to let my deeper meaning set in. She blushes, right on cue. 'Come to my party this weekend.'

'That's it?'

I nod, still holding her eyes.

She bites her lip, thinking about it. 'You know I'm not really into the party scene.'

'I know. But it's kind of an annual party and the guys will freak if I'm not there. Having you there will actually help me. And we'll hang out, talk, like last time. Getting outside your comfort zone might be good for you.'

She considers it, still chewing on her bottom lip. 'How would me being there help you?'

I fight off a smile. Clearly she has no clue about the theme of Delta Sig's next party. 'Oh, it will, don't worry.'

'I suppose I could. I'm sure Madison and Noah wouldn't mind coming too.'

'Of course. Bring your friends.' With my next meeting with her already secured, I feel at ease. Avery has me smiling more than I have since my mom's suicide attempt. Thank fuck for that. I was like a walking zombie for a while there. 'Should we discuss our journaling assignment from class?'

'Sure.' She shrugs and pulls out her syllabus.

My ploy to get her to open up her journal – the one where she wrote a freaking novel about me – is foiled. It remains safely tucked inside her bag.

She slides the sheet of paper toward me and points. 'We have to write entries on our own body image, what attracts us in the opposite sex, and an entry on sexual preferences and orgasms.' Her eyes dart up to mine and she drags her teeth across her bottom lip.

Fuuuck, that's sexy.

Avery stuffs the paper back into her bag, muttering to herself, 'A section on orgasms -- that'll be a short chapter...'

Holy shit. 'What?' I can't help but react. Has no one touched this beautiful girl? Sign me up. Right fucking now.

Her head snaps up. 'I'm just going to shut up now.'

'That's probably wise.' Otherwise I can't be held responsible for bringing her to orgasm myself. Under the table. Immediately.

Avery collapses, burying her face in her hands.

I can't resist reaching over to rub her back between her shoulder blades. 'Hey, it's okay. If you need tutoring in the bedroom too, babe, just ask.'

Avery lets out a groan, and I can't be sure, but I think a string of curse words too. Once her tirade is out of her system, she takes a deep breath and sits up straight. Her expression is still pinched, like she can't believe she told me that.

I push her coffee toward her again, trying to downplay it, and Avery accepts the cup, taking a sip.

'Hey, it's nothing to be ashamed of, but no wonder you're so cranky. I would be too without regular orgasms,' I say.

Avery spits her coffee across the table, choking and sputtering. I scoot my chair closer and pat her back, nursing her back to health until she can clear her stubborn airway.

She grips the table and sucks in a ragged breath, her eyes watering with the effort.

'I'm sorry, Whistle.' I continue rubbing her back. 'I shouldn't have said that. I meant every word, but I'm sorry you got choked up.'

'I didn't get choked up. I choked. Big difference. And don't call me Whistle.' Avery stands, grabbing for her backpack. 'We're done here.'

My hand on her wrist stops her. Maybe I went too far. But I think she secretly likes me pushing her. I lift the bag and place the straps carefully on her shoulders. 'Remember, Saturday. You already agreed.'

'I'll be there.'

Chapter 8

Avery

I stand before the full-length mirror in my dorm, Madison and Noah grinning like idiots at my reflection. 'I can't believe I'm doing this. I'm going to get arrested wearing this in public.'

Madison rolls her eyes. 'First, it's not public; we'll be in the Delta Sig house. And second, it's a pimps and hoes party. You won't get in if you're not dressed the part.'

Of course Jase had left out that vital little piece of information when he challenged me to attend. Madison and Noah were game for going and had filled me in on the party's infamous theme. They helped with my outfit: a black corset top that I am spilling out of – keeping me on constant nipple patrol – and a tiny pair of black boy shorts that show off generous portions of butt cheeks. *Awesome.* My main problem, though, is that the girls are on full display. *Good Lord.*

'That's a lot of boobage,' I say, attempting to tuck them further into the corset.

Madison slaps my hands. 'Don't you dare. You're one of the few girls who can actually pull this outfit off.'

'Tell that to my jiggly ass.' I make a point of looking behind me, like it's somehow offended me.

'Asses are supposed to jingle. Shush.' To demonstrate, she grabs a fistful of my behind and gives it a gentle squeeze. 'Damn girl, I want to skin you and wear you.'

A giggle escapes despite my nerves. 'That's a really disturbing visual.'

Madison and Noah, ever creative, are doing a role-reversal thing. Madison is wearing a leather jacket, black pants, pimp cap with a feather and several heavy gold chains. Noah, her ho, dons only a pair of bedazzled briefs and a glittery bare chest. It's actually hilarious, despite the fact that I'm having a panic attack.

I tug the little shorts lower on my hips. I'm willing to show an inch of stomach if it means my butt is contained.

Noah laces up his red running shoes that happen to look ridiculously adorable with his sparkly briefs. 'Don't get me wrong, I'm happy we're doing this. But why are we going to the Delta Sig party tonight?' he asks.

I hadn't exactly told them about the whole Jase thing, but now might be time to come clean. 'Jase invited me. We've been hanging out a little. Plus, I'm trying this new fun, carefree side like you guys have always wanted.'

'Avery 2.0. Nice.' Noah nods.

Madison's head whips in my direction. 'What do you mean you've been *hanging out* with Jase-the-manwhore-Owens?' Of course that's the piece of information she zones in on. She adds a few more gold chains to her outfit. 'Girls don't just hang out with him. If said hanging out involves getting in a good mattress workout, then yeah…' She waves her hand in my general direction. 'But this…not so much.'

'God. Madison, those romance novels have corrupted your brain. Guys and girls can just hang out.'

Her eyebrows dart toward the ceiling. 'So he hasn't tried anything?'

I shake my head. 'Nope.' *Is that so strange?*

'Nothing? Not even like accidently brushing your boob with his arm?'

'No Madison. And I don't want a guy whose sole mission is to get in my panties. That's *not* a turn on.'

She looks at me like I've grown a second head. 'Then what is a turn on for you?'

Intelligent conversation, healthy debates…those are the things sure to kick start my libido, if my time with Jase is any indication. 'A guy trying to get into my *brain*,' I return.

She laughs. 'So the question is…who's occupying space in that brain of yours?'

Good question indeed. I remain quiet, unwilling to acknowledge, even to myself, that my friendship with Jase might be a bit unconventional. That I might want a tiny bit more. Of all the guys to be interested in…Dumb, Avery, I silently curse myself.

'Noah, seriously…help me out here?' Madison pleads.

He shakes his head. 'Sorry, babe. It's true. You're in uncharted territory here. Jase isn't exactly known for keeping his dick in his pants this long.'

They're ridiculous. I've hung out with Jase a handful of times – one of them in a classroom. Do they really think he just whips it out whenever, wherever? And why does the thought of him handling himself make my stomach do a little flip? Sheesh. I need to pull myself together if I'm supposed to face Jase in this…outfit. Who am I kidding? Outfit is too generous a term for this. A few scraps of fabric covering the important bits do not constitute an outfit. Yet, I dutifully slip into the heels Madison has supplied and teeter out the door after my friends.

Lord help me. I'm going to fall on my ass. And then my ass will fall out of my pants. Disaster city.

When we reach the party, the line to get inside wraps around the side of the house, and I see that my outfit isn't so outlandish after all. It's like each girl took it upon herself to reveal her inner slut tonight. It's disheartening, but since I have no room to talk,

I huff my exposed ass up the front walkway and wait at the door to be let in. Unlike the last time, there's a bouncer manning the door. I recognize him as Jase's friend Trey, but considering he's only looking at my chest, I doubt he recognizes me. He steps aside to let me and Madison inside, but stops Noah at the threshold. 'Whoa bud. Sorry. You're not getting in.'

Noah's outfit is certainly untraditional, but Trey isn't budging, not even as Madison launches in to a tirade about sexism and equal rights. *Good Lord.*

'Hey, I don't make the rules; I just enforce them.' Trey smiles at Madison. 'Hot chicks only.'

I remember Jase punching his number into my phone at the coffee shop and fish it from the tiny handbag Madison secured to my wrist. 'Guys, let me call Jase. He'll get us in.' The fact that I have his phone number earns me another suspicious glare from Madison.

I step to the far end of the porch, distancing myself from the dull-roar coming from inside. It rings several times and just as I'm about to hang up, Jase answers.

'Whistle? Is that you?'

I ignore the idiotic nickname. 'Yeah, it's Avery. We're here, but we can't get in.'

'Shit. I'm in the back removing a couple of over-drunk assholes. Don't leave. I'll be right there.'

Seconds later, Jase appears at the door just long enough to exchange a few terse words with Trey. Trey barks something back in response, and Jase's eyes flash to Noah. Ever the drama queen, Noah cocks a hand on his hip, daring them to comment on his outfit, or lack thereof.

'Whatever, just let them in,' Jase says, then turns to me. 'Find me later,' he calls before disappearing back through the sea of bodies.

*

It's been fifty-four minutes since I last saw Jase. I hate that I know that. I hate how aware I've become of his presence in a matter of a few short days. I nurse a cup of beer, mostly to keep Madison and Noah off my back, and stand with them in the crowded living room. My ass has been grabbed at least half a dozen times and beer spilled down the front of my corset twice. I want to leave. But first I want to see Jase again. *Traitorous body.*

The music's too loud for real conversation, so I sway next to Madison, trying to ignore the way these heels pinch my feet. *Who needs all ten toes anyway?*

I feel Madison's sudden tug on my hand. 'Jase's looking at you like he wants to taste your sweet honey.'

I nearly spit out my drink and break into a coughing fit, sputtering and gasping for air. 'God, Madison.'

But when my eyes find his, holy shit, it's like all the air's been sucked from the room. Jase looks incredibly sexy in his black tailored suit and he's looking at me. Just me. In a crowded room full of people – more than half of which are beautiful sorority girls, wearing next to nothing, clamoring for his attention.

Jase's hot gaze slips from mine, down my chest, caressing my hips, my bare thighs, taking in my sky-high black heels before slowly gliding up to meet my eyes once again. My heart jumps inside my chest, breaking into an all-out sprint, as I realize he makes no apology about checking me out.

I'm suddenly thankful for Madison's intervention and making me wear this outfit, and offer up a silent prayer of gratitude for Victoria's Secret and the corset hoisting the girls up for display. I've never felt so wanted in my entire life. So beautiful and desirable.

Noah leans closer. 'Damn, he looks like he's going to eat you alive. Go talk to him.' He gives me a gentle shove in Jase's direction and I stumble on shaky legs across the room.

Silently, I curse my friends as I make my way through the crowd. I thought they were anti-Jase, but now they're plotting to bring us together. And though I've wanted to see him since I first got here, now I suddenly need a minute. It was sweet of him to make sure we got into the party okay, and I realize I should thank him. I think I like his sweet side. But when I finally stop in front of him, sweet Jase is nowhere to be found. His gaze is deep and penetrating, and I can't help but think he looks angry about something. Really angry.

'Jase?' I question, my mouth suddenly dry.

'Come with me.' He interlaces our fingers and tugs me toward the stairs. We fight our way through the crowd with Jase leading the way. He keeps my hand tightly locked in his until we reach the door to the stairwell. He produces a set of keys, unlocks it, then guides me up, keeping his hand at the small of my back as I ascend the stairs in front of him.

What the heck is wrong with him? I came to his stupid party, even dressed the part. Why does he look like someone murdered his puppy? He doesn't say a word, but his firm hand curls around my hip as he guides me toward the attic.

When we reach his bedroom, he firmly closes the door behind us, before slowly turning to face me. His deep blue eyes radiate intensity, and his expression is nothing like the relaxed, friendly look I'm used to. My blood pumps wildly in my chest, my pulse keeping pace with the beat of the music I can hear faintly from downstairs.

He strips his jacket from his shoulders, and tosses it on a chair beside the door before yanking the knot of his black tie to loosen it, then works on his shirtsleeves. His once crisp white shirt is now undone at the neck and rolled to his elbows. I stand there, feeling over-exposed and confused.

He stalks toward me, caging me in against the wall, his hands resting near my head. I can see the veins in his forearms straining against the skin, and his hands are curled into fists.

'Jase?'

'I was afraid of this.' His voice is low, rough.

'W-what?' I stumble over the simple word with him so close. I can feel his warm breath on my lips, his body heat, and the raw sexiness oozing off him.

'Avery, look at you.' His eyes lower, sending me into a full-body blush.

'What?' It's apparently the only word in my vocabulary.

He meets my eyes and his expression softens, the anger I sensed earlier giving way to something else entirely. 'You're stunning. So lovely.' His hand cups my jaw and his thumb softly brushes against my skin. 'You look amazing in jeans and a T-shirt. In this, you look downright sinful.'

'Jase…' I whimper.

'You're going to kill me with that outfit, doll.'

I look down at myself and frown. 'I'm sorry…' I tug at the shorts again, as if sheer will make them longer.

'Fuck, babe. Don't be sorry.' Jase's eyes search mine, asking for what, I don't know.

But he can have it. Anything he wants.

God, I hate myself.

His hand leaves my jaw only to trail down my throat with gentle pressure. The simple contact steals my breath and desire races through my system. Jase is making me feel things I swore I wouldn't. Shouldn't. Can't.

'Where have you been hiding these beauties?' His fingertip glides along the tops of my breasts, brushing along the edge of the lace.

Apparently Jase has discovered my boobs. 'Boobs are icky,' I blurt. *Kill me now.*

His mouth twitches at my comment. 'I disagree. There's nothing icky about you, babe.' His voice is thick and I'm wondering where the hell cool, confident Jase has gone because the guy in front of me is all nerves and intensity.

His hand slides down my spine, pulling me closer. My body responds as if saying, yes I'm yours. My chin turns up, my tongue dampens my lips, and my pelvis tilts toward his all in a heartbeat's time. Jase's head drops so our lips are aligned, but he doesn't go any farther. His breathing is shallow, too fast, much like mine.

Chapter 9

Jase

I need get my control back before I do something stupid and try to kiss her. If I do that, I won't be able to stop. Turning away, I adjust myself in the suit pants. 'I got you something today.'

'You did?' I hear the smile in her voice, and I'm at least grateful that things aren't weird between us now. She follows me across the room to my dresser. I pull open the top drawer, then point to the bed. 'Sit.'

She does.

'And close your eyes.'

Her lips curl into a smile and her eyes drop closed. She makes a grabby motion with her hands. 'Gimme.'

I chuckle and place the small object in her palm and with her eyes still closed, her fingers explore. 'A whistle.'

She smiles up at me and the urge to kiss her is so strong, I take a step back. 'If you need anything, you just blow that, and I'll come find you.'

Her expression gets soft and she grips the whistle in her hand. 'Where were you when I was in high school?' she asks, her voice just above a whisper. She looks down at the silver whistle in her hands and I can tell her thoughts are far away.

What happened to turn her into this sad, broken girl? Not kissing her was the right move. 'Trust me, you wouldn't have liked me then.'

The air hangs heavily around us, the music faintly audible from the party below, and Avery remains sitting in the center of my bed. But since I know I can't kiss her, I need to get my thoughts back on track.

I loop the red string over her head so the whistle rests between her breasts. 'Should we go back downstairs?'

She gives me a tight nod.

Avery

'What's with the whistle?' Madison asks once I re-join her and Noah in the living room.

'Don't ask.' It makes no sense, even to me, and I know it would make even less sense to someone else. It's Jase's way of showing me he's looking out for me. Even if it is ridiculous.

When I finally spot him again, he's standing across the living room with Stacia. *Ugh.* She's in a figure-hugging red cocktail dress and they're in what appears to be in an intense conversation. Their faces are just inches apart; her hand rests on his forearm and he's bent down speaking near her ear, his voice low and controlled.

She looks up at him, bites her lip and nods. Are they making a plan to meet up later? I want to blow the damn whistle and call interference so bad my entire body is shaking. I want to see if Jase will really come running to me. But I do no such thing. I just stand there, numb, watching their way too comfortable interaction. Her body angles toward his, and his hand brushes her lower back. They look very familiar together.

When she sees me, a practiced smile graces her features. When Jase notices what caught her attention – me gaping at them – he quickly pulls her by the arm around the corner.

Whoa.

What the hell was that and why do I feel the need to punch something? We're just friends, I remind myself. He can talk to whomever he wants.

Noah is dancing with a group of sorority girls, and deciding he won't miss us, I drag Madison into the kitchen. 'I need something to drink.' I lift my cup so she understands over the music.

She nods happily and follows me. I need something stronger than beer tonight. I don't know if it's this stupid outfit that *soo* isn't me, or the fact that I just saw Jase go off with Stacia, but my hands are shaking.

It's not like he's mine. Who he goes off with should be none of my concern.

Jase ventures into the kitchen, alone this time, and watches me and Madison wait at the counter while one of his frat brothers pours us each a shot. I lift the glass to my lips and drop my head back, letting the liquor burn a path down my throat. Why isn't he with Stacia?

'Another,' I tell the guy.

He grins and dutifully refills my glass while Madison shoots me a surprised look. Jase is watching me and I want him to feel the same confusion and helplessness I just felt watching him with Stacia. I down the second shot and slam the glass down on the counter. My eyes tear up and I'm not sure if it's from the liquor or the strange emotions flooding my system. It's been so long since I let myself be interested in a guy, and he's the absolute worst choice I could have made. I should walk away from him right now. That would be the smart thing to do.

'Enough,' Jase growls beside me, his fingers clutching the exposed skin of my hip, pulling me back from the counter.

I glance around, making a show of it. 'Where's Stacia?'

His eyebrows pull together. 'She left. Wasn't feeling well.'

He's smooth, I'll give him that. He stands over me; his presence alone sending chills of awareness through my body. I wave him off. 'Give me another,' I say to the cute blond guy holding the bottle.

Jase steps closer, intensity rolling off him in waves. 'What are you doing?'

Madison glares at him. She doesn't trust him any farther than she could throw him. His good deed of getting Noah inside earlier is obviously forgotten.

'I'm doing what we talked about…little challenges to get outside my comfort zone. What's the problem?' I tap the shot glass against the counter, waiting for my next pour.

Jase's gaze dares the poor guy to pour me one and see what kind of crazy is unleashed. If I was him, I wouldn't pour me one either. 'Fuck, Avery.' He grips my hand, towing me from the kitchen.

I stumble along behind him through the crowded dining room, the two shots already hitting me. Jase pulls open the sliding door and the cool night air is a welcome reprieve. It cools my flushed skin and clears my head the tiniest bit.

He slides the door shut behind us, the music causing the glass to vibrate softly. Without any pretenses, Jase stalks forward. He cups the nape of my neck and angles my mouth to his, before leaning in to kiss me. His mouth is soft at first, but when I kiss him back, he groans low in his throat and coaxes my lips apart to deepen the kiss. His tongue touches mine and all sense of right and wrong is lost. This is heaven. His other hand finds my butt cheek, and gives it a none-too-gentle squeeze. I can feel everything in this one kiss… how much Jase wants me, how badly I wish I could do this… My brain is screaming at me to stop, but my body begs me to continue.

Jase

Her mouth is soft and damp and the way her tongue flirts with mine makes me instantly hard again. Her tongue glides along mine and she balls my shirt in her fists. Her ass fits perfectly in my hand and I grip it, holding her firmly against me so she can feel exactly what she does to me.

Avery plants her hand against my chest and breaks the kiss. 'Jase.' Her eyes are alight with passion, her voice breathless…but her tone is all wrong. 'We have to stop.'

I reluctantly pull away and meet her eyes. They're blazing green and swimming with emotion. Shit. I don't know what I did wrong – and whether to apologize or hush her fears with more kisses. This is why I didn't kiss her earlier. I shouldn't have taken it that far. But Avery arouses in me things I've never felt. It's insane. She's not even mine, and I'm acting like an over-protective alpha male.

She swallows and pulls in a deep breath, the confusion on her face fading. 'I'm sorry.'

I take another step back. 'It's okay. I shouldn't have rushed you.'

Avery shakes her head. 'I'm not even close to being ready.'

Shit. I could punch myself. I've read the situation between us totally wrong. 'On a scale of one to ten, ten being you're ready to rip my clothes off…'

She bites her lip. 'I'm like a negative six.'

'Shit. That bad, huh?' I take a sniff of my armpit, and she laughs. It's so good to hear her laugh and I relax just a bit.

'It's not you,' she says, still smiling. 'How could it be?'

I pull her into my arms, and kiss her forehead softly. 'I'm not going to rush you. When you're ready, you let me know.' I want her. And I will have her. I just have to figure out what's going on in that pretty little head of hers.

She nods wordlessly, but returns my hug, bringing her arms around my neck. 'Thank you. I just…I like what we have.'

I look down at her. 'Me too.'

'Can we just…focus on being friends?'

'Friends.' *Great.* 'Of course.' *Blue balls, here I come.*

I release her and she steps away from me. Friends apparently don't rub their erections against their friend's stomachs. My bad.

53

'I…I need to go,' Avery whispers. I watch as she ducks her head and disappears inside.

Shit fuck.

Sometimes she seems so innocent….and then other times, not. The way she took those shots like a pro, and the way she kissed, that was anything but novice. Her tongue met mine, thrust for thrust, and we moved together effortlessly. There was nothing timid about her then. Blood flow is still directed south as my body struggles to regulate.

I can't figure this girl out. And I want to. Hell, I need to. When I'm with Avery I don't think about the pile of crap that is my life. How crazy everything's become. She's like the fresh start I didn't even know how badly I needed.

Chapter 10

Avery

After class, Jase stops me on the sidewalk, placing his hand on my lower back and leaning close. 'Come home with me,' he says, his ridiculously pretty blue eyes making it impossible to look away.

My mouth twitches and Jase laughs. 'Not like that. I mean we'll study, come up with our strategy for your upcoming assignments. Being a life coach is a big responsibility and I want to make sure I do right by you.'

I do have some homework to do. And Jase's bed is super comfortable. I don't want to second-guess and overthink every decision I make. We can do this as just friends. Friends study together. 'Lead the way.'

Before I can even question it, I'm falling into step beside Jase. Being near him is increasingly throwing me off. I'm distracted watching the way his long, lean form does amazing things to a pair of jeans and a thermal tee when I realize I've almost stepped out into the street.

Oops.

He takes my hand in his, weaving his fingers between mine. The warm, calloused weight of his palm is new and electrifying. It sends a tingle up my arm and into my chest. I file that under Information Jase Does Not Need to Know. 'Is this really necessary?' I make a point of looking down at our joined hands.

55

'Since you seem oblivious to oncoming traffic? Yes. Yes, it is.'

I arrange my mouth in a polite smile to avoid snapping at him. I'd underestimated the distance of one car at that last crosswalk, and suddenly he thinks I need a helmet. I roll my eyes at Jase, but keep my hand within his.

Once inside Jase's room, he turns on some music from his laptop and plops down next to me, making the mattress dip.

The music is soft in the background, but soulful and deep. I like it. 'What's this? A study playlist?'

He shakes his head. 'A playlist? Nah. It's the Black Keys. I buy whole albums, not individual songs. I'm not afraid of commitment, babe.'

I smirk at his strange innuendo. 'Good to know.'

We arrange various books and study implements across the bed, lying side by side on our stomachs. Studying with Jase is pointless. I can't concentrate with him so close, but it's much more entertaining than studying alone in my dorm.

After a few minutes, I look up to find Jase watching me. He's abandoned his psych homework and is watching as I nibble on the end of my pen, trying to decipher my sociology assignment.

I remove the pen from my mouth. 'Hi.'

'Hi.' His voice comes out too high and he clears his throat, and tries again. 'Hi.' Deeper this time.

Gosh, you could cut through our sexual tension with a knife.

'I'll be right back.' I rise from his bed, needing a moment to myself to collect my thoughts. 'Is there a bathroom I can use?'

'There's one just down the steps, second door on the left.'

'Kay.' I start for the door, and Jase stops me.

'Actually, let me come with you and scope things out. It's probably due for a cleaning.'

'Oh, okay.' I want to tell him I'll be fine and don't need a chaperone, but knowing how truly disgusting this house is, he's probably right. A dozen guys sharing a bathroom…*ew*…I shudder at the thought.

Jase directs me to wait in the hall while he cleans up. I hear the bottles of cleaners being sprayed and the sounds of Jase hastily shoving things into drawers. His friend Trey walks by just in time to get hit in the face with a stray T-shirt Jase tosses from the bathroom. 'Get your shit out of here, man.'

Trey catches the shirt and frowns. 'What the fuck are you doing?' he asks, like seeing someone clean is the strangest thing he's ever witnessed. Heck, maybe it is given the state of this house. 'The cleaning lady's coming tomorrow,' Trey adds.

'I know,' Jase returns. 'But Avery needs to use the bathroom.'

Trey chuckles to himself. 'I didn't think it was possible to be pussy whipped when you're not even getting any pussy, but you just proved me wrong.'

My cheeks burn pink and I look down at my shoes, thankful Jase didn't hear that. Jase emerges a few moments later.

'Okay, all yours,' he says.

I mumble my thanks and flee inside the bathroom.

I'm not even sure how it started, but for the past two weeks, Jase and I have been talking on the phone every night before bed. I haven't seen him outside of our human sexuality class and the quick coffee dates we have after class, but I know I'm getting too close. Jase has continued issuing challenges and I brazenly accept. So far, they've been innocent – flirting with the guy at the coffee shop, sleeping naked when I admitted being undressed makes me uncomfortable, things like that.

Jase stirs up feelings I can't process. He gives me courage and strength I haven't felt in the longest time. It's like I can handle anything – take on the world – or maybe just deal with the stuff in my own small world, but either way, I like it.

But tonight, as I lie in bed all snuggled up, listening to Jase's deep voice coming through the phone, I suddenly tense. He's asked me to do something I don't know if I can. He's challenged me to contact the adoption agency to get my records. I'm silent while I weigh the decision. On the one hand, it's something I've thought about doing the last few years, and I like how my conversations with Jase push deeper than the surface level crap I talk about with most people. But I don't know. Once I've seen what's in those files, I can never go back to not knowing. Right now I can romanticize the idea of my birthmom – she could be a supermodel, a senator for all I know. But what if the truth isn't as pretty? What if she's horrible and wants nothing to do with me? Can I live with that?

'Avery? You still with me?' Jase whispers.

I swallow the lump that's taken up residence in my throat. 'I'm here. Just…thinking.'

He releases a sigh and waits me out. A moment later, my voice leaves my body, independent of my head, ranting, rambling, but I can't stop it now. 'What would I do, track her down, show up out of the blue and say, 'Hi, did you give a baby up for adoption nineteen years ago?' That sounds freaking terrifying. What if she's crazy and horrible? What if she wants nothing to do with me? Maybe I'm safer not knowing.' I bite my lip, waiting for him to confirm I'm as crazy as I feel.

He chuckles softly into the phone. 'Relax, babe. Breathe.' I pull in a deep breath, making sure it's audible over the phone for his benefit, and Jase continues. 'I think you'll regret it if you don't. I could come with you…if you want.'

'You'd do that?'

He's quiet for a second. 'Of course I would.'

'Why would you do that? You hardly know me.'

'So.'

'So…she probably lives across the country for all I know.'

58

'Lucky for you I like road trips. Besides, if I'm your life coach, it's my responsibility to see you to her doorstep safe and sound. It's practically part of the job description.'

I don't say anything for several minutes as the meaning of his words sink in. I swallow a wave of emotion. Jase has been nothing short of amazing, and we've only known each other a couple of weeks. I still find it odd that he's appointed himself my life coach, but it's also totally endearing. His gesture is too much, and it's in these moments with him that I feel like I could actually be whole again.

I can hear him breathing, so I know he's still there. 'And if she's horrible, I'll take you out for ice cream, hold you, let you cry on my shoulder, whatever you need, babe.'

Holy. Crap.

'Let me sleep on it,' I whisper.

'I don't want to push you to do something you don't want. I just thought maybe you needed a little shove. And I'll be there with you. I'll help however you want me to.'

No one in my life had ever really encouraged me to explore my adoption in this way. Even my best friend in high school, before she jumped on the Avery-is-a-disgusting-whore bandwagon, thought it was a bad idea. My dads were awesome, she argued. I had cooler parents than anyone. My birthmom didn't want me, so why should I waste my time worrying about her? Yet there wasn't a single childhood memory that wasn't soured by the feeling my mom missed out on it. I always thought of her during major life events, birthdays, holidays, graduation, prom, and, of course, the silent nothingness of Mother's Day. I also thought of her during insignificant moments, like studying myself in the mirror and wondering which of my features I got from her – and to a lesser extent, my birthfather. Since I had the love of two dads, he wasn't the one I missed, despite never knowing. That hurt was reserved just for her.

I wondered if her nose was tiny, upturned and dotted with freckles like mine. Or if I got my green eyes and reddish hair from her. Did she know how to style this frizzy hair? My dads had always been clueless, though they'd dragged me to several hair stylists, trying to help.

I wondered about my first six weeks of life. Was I a bad baby? Why exactly did she choose what she did? Was it a hard, gut-wrenching decision, wrought with pain, or did she just know it was what she needed to do, and did it, unemotionally? My dads claim I was a perfect baby, that I rarely cried or fussed, but still, I wonder about my life before they got me.

'Okay,' I say softly, surprising myself. 'I'll do it.'

'Yeah?' He's smiling.

'Yeah. I'll request the records. As for actually searching for her…maybe…'

'Hey, it's a start. I like it. What do you need me to do?' I hear his bedsprings creak, like he's ready to spring into action if needed. That thought makes me smile.

It takes me a second to respond – the image of Jase in bed is a teensy bit distracting. I imagine his long form stretched out against the mattress, and my body warms as desire, unbidden and uninvited, pools between my legs.

'Nothing,' I say finally. 'All I have to do is email the agency and fax in a sheet with my signature. I already researched it on their website last year.'

'I'm proud of you, Whistle.'

'Thanks.' I'm proud of me too. 'Night, Jase.'

'Night, doll.'

I fall asleep with a smile on my lips, contentment in my heart and questions in my head.

Chapter 11

Jase

It's been several days, but I haven't asked Avery if she's emailed the adoption agency or faxed in the information release. I am serious about helping her. Why wouldn't I be? Even if my own parents are messed up most of the time, I love them and everyone deserves to know who brought them into this world. Even if it does make me nervous to think about what kind of mother gave a sweet little thing like Avery away. Still, I don't want to hassle her. I just want her to be happy. Little by little, I'm watching her blossom and it's beautiful. She doesn't seem to be hiding quite as much, her eyes are bright and determined, and she's even excited about going out this weekend. It's no longer like pulling teeth to get her to come out. Though I know if I push too hard, too fast, I could lose her.

This weekend one of my frat brothers is playing at a local club and everyone is going to watch him perform. I wouldn't mind having Avery alone at my house, but she seems excited about going.

I tell her I will pick her up, amazed that she's set on doing this even without the safety net of her friends. Apparently, they have some theater party tonight. But I like that she trusts me. I stop in front of Avery's dorm, where she's waiting on the sidewalk. Her face lights up when she sees me. It's strange to me that she

61

wouldn't kiss me, yet she clearly feels something when I'm around. This girl keeps me guessing, that's for sure.

Before I can even exit the car to go around and open her door, Avery's sliding in next to me.

'Hi, beautiful.'

Her eyes widen and her mouth curls upward. I don't know who scared her away from male attention, but it's clear she's hungry for it now. 'Hi,' she returns.

'Ready to listen to some bad folk music?'

'Sure. I love bad folk music.'

'Then you're in for a treat.'

We sit through two warm-up bands before my buddy Sloan makes his way to the stage. Our table of a dozen or so stands up and cheers for him. Avery does too, clapping and whistling with the rest of us. Sloan slouches on a stool and begins to strum a familiar cord. Just a man and his guitar – it's a brave move. I've heard him play at the house, but never perform like this. His voice joins the notes and he's actually decent.

Halfway through the set, Avery taps my knee. 'I'm just gonna run to the restroom.'

'I'll take you.' I rise with her.

She gives me a confused look, but nods.

I tell myself it's because she's so innocent and since I brought her here, she's my responsibility to look after. But I know it's more than that. I want every other guy in this place to know she's with me. I rest my hand on her lower back and escort her through the bar. If I could create a sign and pin it on her back, I would. It would say *back the fuck off, she's with me*.

I walk Avery to the back of the club and wait in the hallway while she's inside the ladies room. When she emerges, I can't resist lacing her fingers between mine and guiding her back to our table, before pulling out her chair and settling down next to her.

After the set, we head to my house and instead of taking Avery directly to my room, where I know I won't be able to behave myself, we hang out with the small group that's gathered in the living room. Due to limited seating, Avery sits on my lap, something that's wreaking havoc on my self-control. I place one hand on her hip and she smiles politely at me. She wouldn't be smiling if she knew the wicked thoughts playing through my mind right now. We're having fun, debating the issue of our school mascot's resemblance to a penis. Hearing Avery say the word penis is a treat. Her mouth pouts in the hottest way, and her cheeks are tinged in pink. Stacia comes in and interrupts. Damn Stacia always ruins all my fun.

The chatter in the room dies down as a roomful of eyes look between Stacia and me, complete with Avery balanced on my lap. *Shit fuck.* This isn't good. I feel Avery stiffen, and my hand involuntarily grips her hip, telling her to stay put. Stacia and I aren't dating anymore. She's just going to have to deal with it. Besides, it's not like I invited her here tonight. I swear, I think she drives by and whenever there are lights on or cars in the driveway, she just comes in.

Stacia walks straight past me, swinging her hips and heads for the kitchen. 'Trey, make me a drink, hun,' she says, luring him after her.

I hate how she thinks men are at her beck and call. Shit, they usually are, but that doesn't make it okay. And Trey's an easy target. He's just horny enough to follow. *Asshole.*

That was Stacia's big complaint of me when she and I dated. I wasn't *attentive* enough for her. Her word, not mine. She doesn't want a boyfriend; she wants a pussy-whipped fool at her beck and call to spoil her rotten. Maybe I'll feel that way about a girl someday, but not Stacia. She's already spoiled enough. For the right person, I'll want to do those things, not be guilt-tripped into them.

Even after Stacia leaves the room, Avery's stick-straight posture tells me she's still uncomfortable. I want to get back to our easy banter. 'I think it's time for your next challenge,' I whisper near her ear, my lips rubbing against her skin.

Avery relaxes in my arms and turns slowly to glance at me, a slow smile forming on her lips. 'What'd you have in mind?'

If I tell her what's really on my mind, I'll get slapped. 'I want you to go talk to that guy over there.' I look pointedly at one of my frat brothers, who's picked up Sloan's acoustic and is butchering the simple notes.

'Done and done.' She smiles and rises from my lap.

As soon as her warm weight is gone, I'm regretting sending her away. But watching her confidence grow is a thing of beauty. I'm riveted watching Avery spark up a conversation with Jared. Maybe this was a bad fucking idea. He continues strumming the guitar, glancing up at her only occasionally, and only to give the briefest of replies.

A few seconds later, she slides back into my lap with a huff. 'Well, that was a letdown. He practically ignored me.' She pouts. 'Aren't these little challenges supposed to be *good* for my self-esteem?'

I can't help but smile. Maybe it was cruel to send her over there, but it was just a stupid dare to see if she'd actually do it. 'Sorry babe. I didn't know you'd actually do it. Jared's one of my brothers and he's seen you in my lap all night – he's not going to make a move on you. He values his face too much.'

'What?' Her confusion is adorable. 'So you chose someone you knew wouldn't talk to me?'

I shrug. 'I can't have another guy touching something I want for myself.'

Her mouth drops open. 'Oh.'

We've been pretending that we're friends, because it's all she's ready for, but she has to know I want more. I consider asking her to kiss me. Her mouth is right there, inches from mine, looking fucking delicious, but I can't. I can't bear to hear her turn me down. I glance up and spot a safe-looking target across the room: a guy who looks like he was raised on whole milk and Flintstone's vitamins. Safe as white bread. I wonder if she'll do it. At least it'd be easier to hear her turn him down. 'That guy…over there.' I point and Avery's eyes reluctantly leave mine to seek the target. 'Kiss him.'

Her confused gaze meets mine. 'No kissing. I told you I'm not ready.'

Shit. Now I feel like a dick. 'Fine. Go talk to him then.' I hold her eyes, wondering what she'll do.

Avery surprises me by glancing his way, and then walking toward him without another word. Something twists inside me.

They strike up a deep conversation, and I silently curse myself. This was my grand fucking plan…to drive her into the arms of another guy? I should punch myself in the face.

I sulk on the couch and watch them. I haven't seen the guy around here before. He actually looks like he'd be a decent guy, but that's beside the point. Avery tosses her hair over her shoulder and laughs at something he says. God damn it, she's actually flirting with him. My stomach clenches. He smiles at her, and I have the sudden desire to knock that smile off his face. I grab another beer and down half of it in a single gulp.

Chapter 12

Avery

Jase is helping me break free from my shell in ways I didn't think were possible. I need to thank him for last night. After his little dare gave me the shove I needed, I talked to Mitch for over an hour at the small party. And since Jase got pretty drunk, Mitch even drove me home. I had to give myself a little pep talk, convincing myself that Mitch was a safer choice. That despite my growing feelings for Jase, his reputation and whatever's still going on between him and Stacia means I need to spread my wings a little. Jase and I are just friends and that is for the best.

I exchanged contact info with Mitch and we may be going out next weekend. We'll see if he calls me.

I dress casually in yoga pants and a fitted long-sleeve tee, throw my hair into a ponytail and set off in search of coffee. I pick up an extra cup for Jase, who's no doubt hung-over this morning, and begin the twenty-minute walk to his house, just off campus. I sip my coffee, letting the sunlight warm my skin. The leaves are changing, bursting in pretty oranges and shades of gold. I'm struck by the notion that the leaves are evolving just as I am.

I daydream as I walk, imagining it might be possible to move forward once and for all, when the images of that night creep into my psyche. Me, posing topless for the camera, with a seductive open-mouthed smirk, my hands and mouth on a certain part of Brent's anatomy, making it obvious who I was and not-at-all obvious who he was. It started off as innocent, and I trusted Brent. Completely. Which was dumb. Beyond dumb. He had a reputation when I met him, but I believed he had changed.

It's exactly why I need to exercise caution with Jase. I need to keep him in the friend zone. His belief in me means everything, but anything more will be simply too dangerous. It's a pity the warning signs flee my mind at the first sight of him.

After knocking at the front door for several minutes, I decide to try the knob, and finding it unlocked, I let myself in. It's probably a little forward surprising Jase like this. I know he's probably still sleeping, but I'm sure he'll be happy to see me, so I put it out of my mind and climb the stairs to his room in the attic.

I knock on his bedroom door and wait. Nothing. No sounds from inside. I smile at the thought of him curled up in his big bed. I don't know if I should just go in or what. I tap again. 'Jase?'

I hear him curse and then his heavy footsteps pad across the room. The door opens just a few inches and Jase peeks out at me with bleary eyes. His hair is rumpled and his clothes appear slept in. 'Avery?'

'Morning, sunshine. I brought coffee. Can I come in?'

His confused gaze bounces from the cup of coffee I'm holding back to mine. The look in his eyes is pure panic. Something is very wrong and my insides tingle with the anticipation of bad news. Jase makes no move to open the door any further.

'Jase?' I question after a heartbeat.

He rakes a hand thoroughly his unruly hair. 'Listen, Whistle… you're not going to be happy, but I promise you, absolutely nothing happened.'

I storm past him into his room and see Stacia stretched out on the small sofa under the window. She's just waking up, and dressed only in one of Jase's T-shirts.

My hands are shaking. I set the coffee down on his dresser so I don't throw both cups at him. He's not my boyfriend. We're not dating, but that doesn't mean I'm any less pissed that he and Stacia…did whatever they did last night. But I'm the one that left with Mitch last night, what did I expect?

Jase stops before me, his eyes downcast at his feet.

Stacia stands and stretches, the shirt lifting to show her pink lacy panties with her movement.

'Stacia, it's time for you to go,' Jase says, his voice tight.

She steps into her jeans and tosses her long blond hair over her shoulder. 'Chillax, hun, I've gotta pee and then I'll go.' She crosses the room and heads out into the hall.

Once she's gone, Jase takes my hands in his. 'I swear to God nothing happened. She got too drunk to drive home last night and I let her crash on the sofa. I didn't touch her. I promise you.'

He's still dressed in his clothes from last night – including his belt. If something did happen between them, why would he have dressed in all his clothes again before going to bed? I don't know if I should trust him, but I want to.

He's still holding my limp hands in his. 'It's fine, Jase. You're free to do whatever…whoever you want.'

'Okay, I know. I just…I want you to know that things really are over between her and me, despite what this looks like. I'm not with anybody right now.'

'Fine,' I say. I don't know whether to be mad at him, myself, or Stacia. There are so many emotions running through my system – anger, hurt, embarrassment – that I don't know what to think. For all my supposed caution in getting involved with Jase, I suddenly realize I've built up our bond in my head into something it's not.

Jase pushes his fingers through his thick hair again, cursing himself under his breath. 'She took a bunch of shots and begged me to let her stay. All I did was give her a blanket and leave her up here. She was passed out when I came to bed a couple of hours later.'

My hands are still trembling. That news conjures up the image of a drunk Stacia hanging all over him, begging him to take her to bed. I don't think for a second that she accidently drank too much and needed to stay. She's much too calculated for that. The urge to hit something is barely contained. 'You know she does this on purpose, right?' I ask.

He shrugs. 'Probably. She likes to mess things up for me.'

I decide then and there I won't let Stacia run me off. I'll stand my ground. If Jase wants me here, I'm staying.

Jase picks up the coffee from the dresser. 'You got me coffee?' I nod.

He pulls me in for a hug. 'Thanks, Whistle.'

I stiffen in his arms. One step forward, two steps back.

Stacia chooses that moment to grace us with her presence again. Jase rolls his eyes at her before turning to me. 'I'm going to take a quick shower. Wait for me, okay?'

'Sure.'

He grabs a towel and some clothes and leaves me and Stacia alone in his room. Damn, this is awkward.

She makes a production of lacing up her strappy heels and organizing the items in her obnoxiously bright orange purse. 'Gosh, I don't even remember what happened last night.' She chuckles, inspecting herself in her compact mirror. 'But I guess that'll happen when Jase is feeding you shots.'

I stay quiet, knowing if I open my mouth, it won't be ladylike. But it takes everything in me, and I repeat a quiet manta in my head. *Don't sink to her level. Don't sink to her level.*

Once Stacia is packed and ready to go, she crosses the room and stops in front of me. 'You know he and I are neighbors back home. We practically grew up together. We have a history that can't be undone.' She studies me silently for a moment, and getting nothing in response, she chuckles to herself and continues on her way.

God! I want to hit something. Preferably her face. My blood is boiling. I pace Jase's bedroom, too keyed up to sit down. Maybe all that caffeine was a bad idea. When I pass by his unmade bed, I can't help but stop and stare at the little wicker trashcan sitting beside the bedside table. If they did have sex last night, that trashcan should contain a condom. I walk closer, my heart pounding and peer down into the wastebasket.

An empty water bottle, a wadded up a receipt from the gas station for a tank of gas and a toy whistle.

No condom wrapper.

A breath escapes my lungs in a whoosh of air, and I sink down onto his bed. It's this moment I realize I like Jase way more than I have any right to. I'm in way over my head.

Chapter 13

Jase

When I return from the shower, Avery is curled up on my bed with my journal from our human sexuality class. *What the...*

'Avery?'

She sets the notebook down beside her. 'I have soft skin? That's it. That's all you wrote?' She shakes her head in mock disgust, not at all self-conscious that I just busted her for snooping.

I cross the room and grab the journal. 'Now you have to let me read yours.'

She smiles. 'No way. Not when all you wrote was that cheesy line. You haven't earned it.'

I sit down next to her. 'Then let me earn it.'

She brings her palm to my cheek and meets my eyes. The banter between us dies away, and I'm left with a longing to my very core. Her eyes linger on my mouth. I've never wanted to kiss someone so bad in my entire life. My heart is pounding painfully in my chest while I wait to see what she'll do next.

She reluctantly drops her hand and moves away from me on the bed. 'Things went pretty well with Mitch last night.'

'Oh, right. Mitch.' *That's just fucking great.* 'My challenge was to talk to him. Not to go home with him.'

She swats my arm. 'All we did was talk. He drove me home and was a perfect gentleman.'

'Good.' *Thank fucking God.* 'Are you seeing him again?'

She lifts one shoulder. 'Not sure. We'll see if he calls.'

'He got the digits?'

She nods, smiling coyly.

Damn. That tiny, inconsequential fact shouldn't make me want to punch something, but it does. I mean, Christ, she walked in to find Stacia in my bedroom this morning and she's being so fucking cool about it. I need to pull it together.

Avery sits on my bed, still watching me, waiting for a reaction. I can't be held responsible for my actions when her mouth is so lush and pink. It's practically taunting me. I stand and place my hands on my hips, needing to infuse some humor into the situation. Otherwise, I'm going to kiss her again, and that clearly isn't what she wants.

'Well, since it seems you're really excelling at the challenges I'm dishing up, it looks like we're ready for something more advanced.' I hope she can't tell I'm literally making this up as I go.

A musical ringtone fills the silence and Avery lunges for her phone. 'Oh, hang on one sec, it might be Mitch.'

Shit fuck.

I lie in bed, still wondering if I handled things right with Avery. I practically pushed her into Mitch's arms last night. But of course that was *after* she told me she wasn't ready for anything. What can he give her that I can't?

Before I call her for our nightly chat, I dial my mom's cell.

She answers on the first ring. 'Jasey?'

I inwardly groan at the nickname. 'Hey, Mom.'

'Hi honey. What's up? Calling to check on me?'

I smile. No use beating around the bush with her. 'I guess so, yeah. How are you?'

'I'm doing fine, Jase. Your dad's going to China on business later this week. He'll be gone for two weeks, so if you wanna come see me…'

We both know that it's a bad idea for me and my dad to be in the same house together. 'Yeah, I will.'

'Well, I really am doing good, honey. I joined a new book club at the library.'

'Good, Mom. I love you.'

'Love you more, Jasey.'

It's a relief to hear her doing so well. I still beat myself up that I didn't see the warning signs before. Not answering her phone and forgetting to call me back for weeks on end, the robotic tone in her voice when we did talk. I should have known something was off. Hell, my dad really should've known something wasn't right. But he ignored her like usual, until he found her in a heap on the bathroom floor. I'd never heard his voice so panicked when he called to tell me she'd been taken by ambulance to the hospital.

'Okay, I'll see you next weekend.'

'Bye honey.'

Looks like I'm going home again next weekend. I switch off the lamp and get comfortable under the sheets before calling Avery. Hearing her sleepy voice right before she falls asleep always makes me grin.

'Hi,' she whispers softly.

'Hi.' We're both silent for a few seconds, but there's nothing uncomfortable about it. 'Did you have fun with Mitch?'

'Yeah. He took me out for hot chocolate and then we just walked around campus for a while.' I can hear the smile in her tone.

Douche. 'Cool. That sounds nice.'

'Yeah, he's a little quiet, so we didn't have much to talk about, but I think it was a good assignment for me.'

'So you're not seeing him again?' I cross my fingers. And my toes.

'I didn't say that. He said something about going out next weekend, so we'll see.'

An idea pops into my mind and now that it's planted itself there, I know I won't be able to shake it. 'Oh, shoot. I was going to ask you to come home with me next weekend.'

She pauses, just the sound of her breathing through the phone as she considers it. 'Really?'

'Yeah. I need to go home to check on my mom while my dad's in China on business. I was going to see if you'd want to come with. My mom's really cool and we could just hang out, watch movies, go in the hot tub. It'd be low key. If you're interested…'
I mentally high-five myself at the pure genius of this solution. It keeps her away from Mitch the Bitch and gets her closer to me all in one fluid motion.

'Ah, yeah, sure. That sounds fun.'

Call it evil genius or exceptional planning on my part, but the fact that Avery is in my car next to me on the three-hour journey to my mom's just feels right. When we pull in to my neighborhood, Avery leans forward in her seat to look out the window. It's a nice neighborhood, I know that. Each house is huge and immaculately maintained; even if they do all look strikingly similar. Too cookie-cutter.

I pull onto the circular brick driveway and park in front of the four-car garage.

'Wow. Nice place.'

The house is way too big for just my mom and dad, part of the reason my mom goes crazy sometimes. I would too, alone in a cold, quiet house. But looks can be deceiving because yes, it's an amazing house. Red brick exterior, fountain out front, pool and hot tub in back, more bedrooms and bathrooms than we'll ever use.

Avery climbs from the car and stretches. 'This is where you grew up?'

'Yep.' I reach into the backseat and grab both of our overnight bags. My mom's waiting for us on the wide front porch, looking at Avery curiously. I realize I've never really brought a girl home before. Stacia doesn't count: she lives three houses down and was always here, invited or not.

I'm happy to see my mom looking put together. There's color in her cheeks and her eyes are bright. Sometimes I wonder if I've been coming home to see her so often to try and erase the memory of her looking so pale and tiny in that hospital bed. She bore no physical scars. Even her suicide attempt had been nice and neat. Able to be swept under the rug and forgotten. How polite of her. We never mentioned the word addiction, even as her use of pain pills for her back increased drastically over the years. And we never used the word suicide. *Mom's accident* was the term my dad coined. Fucking prick. No wonder she didn't know how to ask for help.

I turn and catch Avery nervously wringing her hands and push all that shit from my head. 'Ready?'

Avery nods and I lead her forward.

Avery

Jase's mom is gorgeous. She's got long dark hair, neatly secured at the nape of her neck, and wide honey-colored eyes with the same thick, dark eyelashes as Jase. Her eyes are weary though, and are currently sizing me up. I wonder what Jase has told her about me. Does she think we're dating?

When we reach the porch, she pulls Jase into a hug, and I wait nervously beside them.

'Avery?' she asks, releasing him.

I nod once. Her smile is wide and welcoming, and I see that I have nothing to worry about. 'Hi, Mrs. Owens.'

'Call me Cathy.' She pulls me in for a hug too, and I hear her tell Jase over my shoulder 'She's gorgeous, Jase.'

He chuckles. 'Trust me, Mom, I'm all too aware.'

I stand there stunned, trying to pretend they're not talking about me like I'm not here, trying to pretend that Jase thinking I'm gorgeous doesn't turn my insides to mush. We enter the house and the inside is even more immaculate than the outside. A large marble floored foyer with a round table holding a giant vase of fragrant peonies greets us. Wow. A staircase winds off one side of the foyer, and the other opens to a spacious living room with the highest ceiling I've ever seen.

Jase gives me a tour of the large, opulent first floor with Cathy trailing behind us, asking us each occasional questions about school. She leaves us after that, saying dinner will be at five, excusing herself to the sunroom where she perches in a lounge chair with a romance novel.

Jase leads me upstairs to his bedroom. The carpeting is so soft and plush beneath my feet as I trail after him down the long hallway. Their house really is beautiful.

His bedroom appears unchanged from high school – the walls are adorned with posters of supermodels and pro athletes, and a shelving unit holds various trophies and medals. When I get closer, I see they're for swimming and tennis. Interesting. I didn't take him for much of an athlete, though his lean physique begs to differ.

He crosses the room and tosses our bags onto a dark mahogany sleigh bed that sits under the window. He doesn't expect me to sleep in here, does he? Surely his mom wouldn't be okay with that. Surely *I* wouldn't be okay with that.

'Jase?' I question, watching him walk toward me.

'I like having you in my space.'

Uncertain of how to answer, I remain still and silent as he approaches. His hand cups my jaw, his thumb skittering back and forth against my skin. My eyes flick to his mouth, lingering on his lips, that I know from experience are incredibly soft and full.

His mouth curves up a fraction and I know I've been caught. His thumb continues its gentle caress on my cheek and his eyes are bright with desire.

'You know this isn't going to work. Should we just get it out of the way?' he asks finally.

'Get what out of the way?'

'Sex.'

'Excuse me?'

'You've got to feel this raw sexual energy radiating between us.'

I scoff. 'I most certainly do not.' *Lie.* My damn panties are probably wet. Bastard.

He laughs, a deep throaty chuckle that lights up my nerve endings and makes my skin tingle. 'Despite your tendency to lie through your teeth about being attracted to me, you're still outrageously delicious.'

'Delicious?'

'Outrageously so.'

'So now I'm outrageously delicious? Isn't that a cereal tagline?'

'No. That's magically delicious. And stop changing the subject.'

'And what subject are we on?' I ask, suddenly breathless.

'The eventual sex we're going to have. I'm going to open you up in more ways than one, babe.'

Holy shit. My knees buckle and I reach out to grasp onto Jase's biceps. 'Jase,' I rasp. If I had any upper body strength I'd punch myself in the ovaries for the idiotic way I'm behaving. But he possesses the distinct ability to turn me into a pile of hormones, and there's no denying that fact.

His eyes have gone dark, all the humor has disappeared from his face. 'Tell me what you want.'

'I can't. I need more time.'

His eyes dart from my mouth to my eyes. 'We'll discuss this later. I'll show you to your room.'

I nod and follow him, being sure to keep my clutch on his arm so I don't stagger on my uncooperative legs.

Over dinner, Jase asks his mom about her therapy appointments and medication dosage, and I'm surprised they're talking so openly in front of me. On the car ride over, Jase explained the reason he needed to check on her – saying that she lost it several months ago and was briefly hospitalized. I'm sure there's more to the story, but not wanting to pry, I allowed him to share only what he was comfortable with me knowing. Lord knew there were plenty of secrets I kept to myself. The fact that Jase has brought me home and introduced me to his mom, someone who's clearly important to him, leaves me feeling rattled. He continues to surprise me with his openness – making himself vulnerable while I stay closed off.

His mom squeezes his hand from across the table, the simple touch meant to reassure. 'I'm on a low dose anxiety pill, but I told you, honey, I really am doing much better. I've been exercising again, gardening a little too. Things are good right now.' She smiles at him, but Jase's face remains serious, guarded, like he's trying desperately to decipher her words.

I sit in silence while his mom heaps a scoop of mashed potatoes and a slice of meatloaf onto my plate. It's nice to have a home cooked meal, and the food smells delicious.

'I'm so proud of my son. I can't believe you're a junior in college already. Your dad and I are both proud,' Cathy says out of the blue. I think she's just desperately trying to change the subject. I know I would be.

'Don't, Mom.'

'I'm serious, Jase. He felt bad about how things went last time you were home.'

Jase shifts uncomfortably in his chair. 'Let's just drop it. I'm sure Avery doesn't want to hear *all* the family bullshit.'

'Jase,' Cathy pleads.

I find his hand under the table and give it a squeeze. 'It's fine.'

I hate seeing Jase uncomfortable, and apparently discussing his Dad sets him off. I want to take the pressure off him, and feeling inspired by how open they've been, I take a deep breath and launch into the story about starting my search for my birthmom. Cathy leans forward, silently encouraging me with the soft crinkles around her eyes. The crease between Jase's brows disappears. It's the first time I've confirmed to Jase that I went ahead and completed the initial paperwork and he grins at me.

After that little sharing session, I focus on my meal, attempting a bite of the meatloaf. It's horribly dry and I force the bite down. Across the table, Jase is doing the same, the lump of food lodged in his throat visible.

Cathy sets her fork down and frowns. 'Sorry, I didn't make any sauce or gravy, you guys. Is it too dry?' she asks.

'No, it's great,' I lie.

She smiles apologetically, like she knows I'm lying but isn't going to call me on it. Jase smirks and takes a gulp of his water to get the bite down.

'Sorry about that meatloaf from hell,' Jase says, slipping into the hot tub next to me. It takes a full minute for his words to register. His chest and abs are sickening. His entire torso is sculpted muscle and I'm a horny, hormonal mess. Crap!

'Hm? Oh, it's fine,' I manage when I realize he's still waiting for a response.

'She's normally a really good cook,' he says, sinking onto the bench seat beside me. He finds my hand under the warm water and gives it a squeeze. Chill bumps rise over my skin, despite the heat vapors drifting lazily around us. 'You're already pruned.' His fingers skim along mine.

'You took forever to change,' I explain.

'Yeah, sorry about that. I went to say goodnight to my mom and wanted to ask again about how she was doing.'

'Oh.' Now I feel guilty, complaining I had to wait in a wonderfully relaxing hot tub while he took care of his mom, probably tucking her in and everything like a good son. A bad boy who loves his mom? Oh Lord, I'm done for. I shift on the bench seat, suddenly finding things a bit cramped with Jase's large form stretched out next to me. There's nowhere to look that isn't his tan, smooth skin, nowhere to move where I won't accidently brush against him.

His grip on my wrist effectively stops my squirming. 'Hey, Whistle. Breathe for me, okay?'

Can he see the panicked look on my face? Hear the pounding of my heartbeat?

I pull a ragged breath into my lungs as Jase slides closer and tips my chin to meet his eyes. 'Tell me what's wrong.'

'You…'

'Me?' His smile falters.

'Not you…but you in swim trunks…'

He looks down at his naked chest, his gaze wandering down to the navy blue board shorts submerged underwater. A slow smile blooms on his mouth as he realizes that his half-naked form is what's gotten me all flustered. 'Babe, you in a bathing suit is a thing of fucking wonder, trust me. But I told you, nothing's gonna happen that you're not ready for.'

A tiny whimper escapes the back of my throat and my eyes slide closed.

Jase is going to think I'm crazy. Hell, I am crazy. I've warned him away from me numerous times, and now I'm ready to beg him to get closer. Far from the pressures of school, in a place where no one knows me and a beautiful man is looking at me with desire in his eyes? There's no way I'll be able to resist. And the thing is, I don't want to. I just want to let go.

His expression is tense, his jaw working as he reads the emotions in my features. 'Whistle…' His hold on my jaw remains, his thumb lightly stroking my cheek. 'Stay still. Let me kiss you.' He moves closer, not waiting for my answer. It must be obvious on my face. His breath mingles with my own as he closes the distance between us. 'Just once,' he whispers.

When my hands move from my lap, I'm not sure. But they tangle themselves in the hair at the back of his neck, and I use the leverage to pull Jase closer. His mouth presses against mine, warm and solid and grounding me in this moment. His lips begin to move, slowly devouring, slowly unraveling what I've worked hard to bury. His tongue glides along mine and a wave of heat tingles on my skin, pooling between my legs. One more soft caress of his tongue swiping against mine, and Jase pulls back to gauge my reaction.

My entire body is humming with pleasure, and I'm ready for more. 'Still with me?' he asks.

I nod, obediently.

His jaw relaxes, and he slouches down into the bench seat, visibly relieved at my reassurance. With one hand still holding mine, he pulls me over to him, nestling me in against his body. Which is good, because without something solid to grasp onto, it's possible I could drown in the three feet of water.

His fingers lace with mine and he releases a heavy sigh. 'Okay… so you liked the kiss.'

I nod.

'And your body was practically begging me to continue…' His fingertips lightly graze my bare thigh. 'Which means I'm completely confused.'

I swallow a wave of nerves, biting my lip but make no move to explain.

'Say it, Avery. Tell me this is okay. You're not like other girls I've been with, and I fucking love that, but I'm totally unsure what to do here.'

I know I've told him I'm not ready, that I don't want this. But what scares me more than anything is that I actually do want this…want him…so bad I can feel it in my core. 'I'm not good at all this. I had my trust broken big time. And I just…'

His hand squeezes mine. 'Hey. It's okay. I don't want to push you. You just…you know how I feel about you, right? You're perfect, Avery.'

Ha! I am so far from perfect, but rather than tear myself down again, I focus on his words, the honest need in his eyes. He doesn't mention the R-word, so I'm not sure if we are talking about a relationship or just the physical aspects. And I still hate his relationship with Stacia more than is even remotely normal. But half-naked Jase is clouding my judgment and I crawl over into his lap, placing my palms on each of his cheeks. 'Kiss me again.'

Several minutes later, I'm moving against his lap and we're still kissing eagerly when Jase pulls back. 'Avery…wait. My mom's bedroom is right up there.' He points to the second floor window looking down on us. 'I think she's sleeping, but just in case…we should go inside.'

I nod, and disentangle myself from his lap. Sheesh. The last thing she needs to see is me wildly riding her son in their hot tub.

Watching Jase get out of the hot tub is a test of my physical restraint. His erection strains against his swim trunks and he tucks a towel around his waist, grimacing as though it's painful. He grips my hand firmly and tows me inside as I let out a giggle.

Chapter 14

Jase

Avery is damp and flushed from the hot water and is lying against my pillow. It is a beautiful sight. She chews on her bottom lip. 'Are you sure your mom won't be mad that I'm in here?'

My mom knew I was sexually active from the time I was sixteen and supplied me with condoms; I'm pretty sure she'd be okay with this. I just nod. 'She won't care. Trust me.'

'Well, I'm not sleeping in here,' she says.

'Whatever you want.'

I lie down next to her, curling my body around hers. She's changed into a pair of little sleep shorts and a tank top, with no bra – which my dick won't let me forget – but I have no plans of pushing her any farther than she wants to go. I'd changed into jeans and a T-shirt, not wanting to be presumptuous. Avery snakes a hand under my shirt and rests her palm against my back. The simple touch from her is highly intimate, knowing how cautious she is sharing anything physical.

She angles her body closer to mine, and I remain still, allowing her to take the lead. She's looking at my mouth again and I know I'm not going to be able to resist. Anchoring one arm around her, I lean down and kiss her. I'm not used to going this slow, hell I'm not used to having a girl in my bed at home after just having dinner with my mom. But I like it. Avery's pouty mouth is so soft against mine, I can't resist deepening the kiss, tasting her again. And when my tongue touches hers, her soft moan punctuates the silence, and desire races through me. Before I have time to consider my next move, I'm on top of her, caging her in with my body, kissing her deeply and crushing my hips against hers. The way Avery moves her body under mine, sliding her hands up and down my back, angling her hips to meet mine is incredible. She's warm and soft and I want more.

She breaks the kiss suddenly. 'Jase, what are we doing?'

My hand freezes over her ribs, feeling her heart ricochet against them. *She wants to talk now?* 'I'm trying to get to second base.' I smile weakly.

She laughs softly, burying her face in my shoulder. 'I meant what is this…with us?'

'What do you want it to be?' I brush the stray hair back from her face.

'I, I don't know,' she admits.

'Okay.' She's not giving me much to go on. 'Do you need me to stop?'

This time her voice is firm. 'No.'

Thank God.

'Now, about that second base.' Her voice is careful and she fixes her mouth in a polite smile.

A smirk overtakes my mouth. This girl is too much. I'd die if she didn't want me to touch her there. Her tits are lovely in the most distracting way possible. I'd barely been able to keep my hands off them in the hot tub, peeking out from the little bikini, but now there's only a thin cotton T-shirt separating us, and she's coaxing me on. Shit, I can feel her nipples rasping against me when she moves.

The little smile still playing at the edge of her lips, Avery lifts her shirt over her head and tosses it to the floor. Holy. Shit. She makes no move to cover herself, though her cheeks hold a hint of heat. Her chest rises and falls heavily with each breath, and her eyes stay glued to mine.

'You're amazing,' I whisper, trailing a knuckle over her collarbone as my eyes travel down. 'So beautiful.'

She swallows heavily and her hands scramble to remove my shirt next. I yank it over the back of my head and toss it to the floor, then lower myself down on her again. Why had I never noticed the brilliance of skin to skin contact? She's warm and soft and still moving against me. This couldn't have been more intimate if I was inside her. Her warm skin rubbing against mine, the rise and fall of her heavy breasts with each breath is enough to undo me.

I lightly trace a fingertip across her nipple while delicately palming her other breast. Avery sucks in a breath and a tiny whimper escapes on her exhale. I'm trying to be soft, careful with her, to make myself go slow. I sense this is a big moment between us, and I don't want to do anything to wreck it. But I've never been this turned on, and I have to fight off the urge to go farther. I'm not used to being this controlled. Her nipples tighten under my touch and her heart is pounding in her chest. I press soft kisses all along her neck, enjoying the feel of her body squirming under mine.

My hands caress and explore and stroke while my mouth seeks hers, devouring, needing to possess her in this one way. For now.

Chapter 15

Avery

In the morning, Jase's mom redeems her cooking abilities by making the most delicious homemade waffles with fresh blueberries. We gather around the table, eating quietly, but I can feel Jase's eyes constantly wandering to me. He and I haven't said much to each other after last night's extremely heated make-out session. I didn't think Jase was used to going too slow, but I was proud we kept things under control. Even though our shirts were off, our pants stayed firmly in place. Which wasn't easy, especially since I could feel Jase's arousal straining against his jeans. Sheesh. I need to keep my mind out of the gutter. I focus on taking another bite of the waffles in front of me.

'So…what should we do today?' Jase asks.

'You guys do whatever you'd like,' his mom answers.

Jase turns to look at me, measuring my reaction.

I shrug, my expression relaxed and open.

'Well, I thought we could hang out with you today,' Jase says to his mom, 'And then tonight I could take Avery out and introduce her to a few of my friends.'

'Yeah, that sounds great. I'm open to whatever.' I feel surprisingly at home and comfortable being with Jase and his mom. There's none of the awkwardness of being a house guest, or trying to force polite conversation just to fill the silences. We'd broken through that pretty quickly last night – gotten into some pretty heavy topics, which Jase navigated us through with ease. He has an easy-going nature about him that makes people feel instantly comfortable. I like being around him. I feel accepted and at ease, which for me is really saying something. These last few years, I haven't always felt comfortable in my own skin, let alone in the company of a guy like Jase. I'm glad I met him and gave him a chance. Despite what I'd heard about his reputation, he's been nothing like the hard-partying, womanizing frat boy that Madison made him out to be. And truth be told, I actually like that he has a past he isn't proud of. It might make it easier for him to accept mine knowing he isn't perfect, either.

I help Jase's mom with the breakfast dishes while Jase does a few chores around the house – changing a light bulb in the garage and replacing a battery in a smoke detector. It feels very natural and homey being here with them. I am thoroughly enjoying the weekend break away from campus and the dorms.

We lie low the rest of the day, relaxing at home with his mom. She makes us lunch and even breaks out Jase's baby albums. He was the cutest, chubbiest, blond-haired, blue-eyed baby ever. Seriously, he could have been a model.

Jase sits in the armchair and frowns while his mom and I huddle together on the couch, flipping through the pictures, giggling and murmuring what a cutie he was. Seriously, he was blessed geneti-cally. I have no doubt that someday he will make beautiful babies.

Jase says the night will be low-key, just a casual get-together at his friend Radar's apartment. Apparently, his friend Steve's last name was Radaresky and everyone had called him Radar since eighth grade. Jase has been friends with this group for years and he tries to visit them whenever he's home for the weekend. They'd chosen to remain in town and get jobs rather than go off to college. He also mentions this is a group of friends his dad doesn't approve of. No wonder Jase is so loyal – it seems he'd do just about anything to defy his dad.

I dress in a pair of skinny jeans and layer a couple of long-sleeved tees on top. The nights are starting to get cooler as fall settles in. Jase meets me in the foyer, looking scrumptious in jeans and a light blue hoodie that brings out the blue in his eyes. Only Jase can make jeans and a sweatshirt look sexy. Sheesh, I'm in trouble.

Jase kisses his mom goodbye. 'We'll be late, Mom, so don't wait up.'

'Okay.' She waves us off.

It's a quick drive across town to an older brick-front apartment building. Jase leads me up three flights and taps on the door in a series of secret knocks before pushing it open. It's interesting to get a glimpse of his life outside the frat house. I like all the sides he's showing me: first, the sweet, caring side with his mom, and now his willingness to introduce me to friends from home.

'Hey!' A scrawny blond guy yells when Jase comes through the door. 'Adonis!' he says, lifting his glass in a mock salute.

'Adonis?' I ask Jase, trailing behind him to enter the apartment.

Jase chuckles and shakes his head. 'Greek god.'

That's right. Adonis was the Greek god for beauty. I can see that. He has a freakin' eight pack for Pete's sake. Not to mention that gorgeous face, piercing blue eyes and his perfectly styled hair that looks like he'd rolled out of bed after a sexy romp. But it's funny to me that even his male friends are aware of his superior status and tease him about it.

He takes it good-naturedly – the look on his face is relaxed and amused. He leads me toward a round felt-lined poker table and toward the group of guys in the middle of a card game. He introduces me to Radar, the wide-smiling blond who called him Adonis; Dave, a shaggy-haired hippie type; Sal, an olive-skinned cutie with a baseball cap pulled low over his eyes; and Matt, a tall red-headed guy with the lightest blue eyes I'd ever seen. They all say hello, but it's obvious we are interrupting their game.

We venture into the living room next, where a guy and girl are playing a video game and another girl sits sulking on the end of the sofa. Jase doesn't introduce me, but I see them exchange a glance that's anything but friendly. I sense they have a past, and as curious as I am, part of me doesn't want to know. I'm already aware of Jase's history with girls, but that doesn't mean I want to sit there while a girl he'd slept with shoots daggers at us with her eyes.

I tug on his arm. 'Can we get something to drink?'

'Sure.' Jase looks relieved to leave the awkwardness behind.

We stand in the kitchen sipping from bottles of beer while the question about who the bitter girl is in the other room remains unspoken on the tip of my tongue. Part of me just wants to ask him, but I hold it in. I'm not dating him and I've told him practically nothing about my past, so what gives me the right to pry?

Jase looks thoughtful, leaning against the counter like he wants to say something. 'The answer to your question is yes,' he says finally.

'What question?'

'You're wondering if I slept with that girl in there.'

Whoa. His honesty levels me. 'And you did?'

He nods. 'In high school.'

'Why are you telling me this?' He doesn't owe me an explanation.

'Because I know you could sense something and I want to be honest with you.'

'Oh.' *Honesty. What a concept.*

'It was only once, drunkenly at a party. I think she was hoping it'd turn into something more.'

I study him, his navy blue eyes, his chiseled rough jawline dusted with light stubble. I can see how girls probably throw themselves at him, hoping it'll turn into more. 'But it didn't?'

He shakes his head. 'I was a dick back then. It was my senior year of high school, and I was getting ready to leave for college. I didn't want to be tied down with a girlfriend; I wanted to play the field. And when she told me she'd always liked me, I assumed she'd be okay with one night…'

While I couldn't relate to exactly what that girl had gone through, I did still know the string of rejection when the guy you'd given yourself to physically didn't value it. 'You should go talk to her. Apologize.'

Recognition crosses his features, but before he can answer, Radar comes strolling into the kitchen. He and Jase share a bro hug – the kind that comes with a hand shake and then a couple of loud pats across the back. Then Radar turns to me.

'Welcome to Radar's love palace.' His hands sweep out in front of him, indicating a tiny messy kitchen, and dim, sparsely furnished apartment beyond. If he believes this is a love palace, I'm certain Radar hasn't seen any action in quite some time.

'Dumbass.' Jase playfully shoves his friend on the shoulder. 'Keep an eye on Avery for a minute. I'm going to talk to Lauren.'

Radar nods. 'Sure thing, boss.'

I don't know what might come of it, but I am proud of Jase for at least trying to make amends with the girl.

Radar grabs a fresh beer from the fridge before surveying me up and down with a smile. 'Jase must be pretty serious about you. He's never brought a girl home for the weekend before.'

I flush pink. 'Oh no, we're just friends.'

Radar laughs, a dimple appearing next to his mouth as his smile widens. 'Trust me. He wants to be more.'

I want to dispute it, but I wonder if Radar could be right. I'm not sure what's going on between me and Jase, only that I like where it's headed.

*

Jase

Avery is quiet on the ride back to my mom's. She spends the drive flipping through the radio stations. I can tell there's something going on inside her head, but I don't pressure her. I know she isn't quite there yet with me, I know she's getting closer to letting me in. Especially after I'd manned up tonight and apologized to Lauren.

Avery and I didn't stay long at Radar's after my conversation with Lauren. It started off awkward, but as soon as I'd uttered the words I'm sorry, her shoulders dropped and she'd instantly relaxed around me. After that, the words just came to me. I told her how I'd used girls as a distraction to escape my home life, and she admitted she learned girls can't trap guys into a relationship simply by getting physical. We talked for about fifteen minutes, each of us more comfortable and relieved by the end of the conversation. I knew things wouldn't be awkward if I ran into her again. The whole experience was a revelation.

Afterwards, I found Avery and Radar where I'd left them in the kitchen, laughing over a story he was telling her. We stayed a little longer, visiting with the guys before calling it a night. The mood changed after my conversation with Lauren, and plus I didn't mind leaving early because the thought of being alone with Avery appealed to me more.

The house is dark and quiet, but I can navigate my way in the dark, so I place a hand on Avery's lower back and guide her to the stairs. Once we're on the landing, I walk her to the door to the guest room and stop, rather than bringing her to my room like I really want to do.

She isn't mine, and last night I probably pushed things too far. And sensing Avery's quiet, contemplative mood on the drive home, I stand silently with her at the door to the guest bedroom.

'I'm proud of you for apologizing to Lauren,' she says finally.

I'm quiet while I watch her. I'm not sure what she wants from me, what she needs. If I did, I'd give it to her, without question. But those sad eyes of hers are hard to read. I lean down and plant a kiss on her forehead. 'Night, Whistle.'

She nods once, blinking those wide green eyes at me, then disappears into the guest room.

Avery

When Jase practically shoves me into the guest room, I'm confused. And hurt. I thought we were really getting somewhere, and after last night's make out session, I'd been looking forward to a repeat of that. Apparently Jase isn't. Which sucks. But I scrub my face, brush my teeth, and try not to pout as I crawl into bed.

In the morning, things are quiet over breakfast again, and Jase doesn't dally – we're soon saying goodbye to his mom and in the car for the journey back.

The closer we get toward campus, the more my panic sets in. Madison had been beyond pissed that I was going home with Jase, not believing for a second that his motives were virtuous with me, and now Jase, the guy I'm risking everything for, is barely speaking to me.

When he parks in front of my dorm, we exit the car and I wait while Jase retrieves my bag.

'I don't know what I did wrong…but I don't want things to be weird between us now,' I say.

His eyebrows draw together. 'You did nothing wrong. I thought maybe I'd rushed you the other night, so I wanted to make sure you knew that wasn't all I wanted.'

Oh. I shake my head. 'Well, you got quiet on me… so I figured you were mad about something.'

His finger presses over my lips. 'Stop thinking so much. I'm not mad. I'm giving you time to sort out whatever you need to sort out. Just don't shut me out, okay?'

I nod. 'Thanks for this weekend.'

'Thanks for being so sweet to my mom,' he says. He leans down to plant a tender kiss against my forehead, then turns back for his car.

I was right about Madison's mood. She sends me suspicious looks and cryptic comments all afternoon while I try to study. I'm relieved when Noah shows up for our regular Sunday night dinner in the cafeteria.

I load my plate with mystery casserole, not able to focus on anything but Madison's suspicions. Am I being stupid to think there's something between me and Jase? When I slide into my seat, Noah has clearly been briefed on my weekend getaway, because he too is scowling at me.

I set my tray on the table, but remain standing in front of them. 'What? Will you two just spit it out?'

Noah places his hand on Madison's, telling her he's got this. 'We just think you need to be careful. Jase could be playing some kind of game with you. And you're bound to fall for him, spending so much alone time with him.'

Maybe I should take their intervention as concern, but for some reason, it just annoys me. 'Is it so impossible that Jase really likes me? How many other girls has he brought home for the weekend to meet his mom? Did you ever think maybe this is something different between us?'

Noah holds up his hands in surrender. 'Alright. We love you. We support you. As long as you've thought it through.'

Madison smiles weakly and I can tell they're mentally deciding to pick up the pieces when I get dumped.

'Fine.' I slide into the seat and stab at the food on my plate. Do they know something I don't? Is this all going to blow up in my face like they think?

By Tuesday afternoon, I'm looking forward to human sexuality class if only to see Jase. Professor Gibbs' lecture is about self-love, i.e., masturbation – a topic I'm decidedly uncomfortable with. Sure, I've tried it, but I don't get the hoopla. He discusses the importance of communication with your partner and part of that effective communication is first understanding your body and its needs. I am so damn uncomfortable during the entire lecture that by the time class is over, I escape out the doors, Jase's deep chuckle making the hairs on the back of my neck rise as he follows me.

I slip into our regular booth while Jase orders the coffee. I get my blushing under control by the time he returns, delivering a cup of coffee to me with a smirk.

He sits down across from me, his eyes playfully dancing on mine. I brace myself for the embarrassing comment he's sure to make from the lecture. Only he doesn't. His eyes grow serious and he leans in toward me, his unique scent of cologne and fabric softener greeting me. 'You sure you're okay with what happened between us last weekend?'

I swallow. 'Why wouldn't I be?' I want to appear, cool, effortlessly sexy, and easy going. Too bad I'm a bundle of nerves, gripping the table in front of me for support, ready to melt into a puddle on the floor with the way Jase is looking at me.

His voice drops an octave lower. 'Because I'm willing to lend my services…to extend your assignments into a gray area I've nicknamed Operation Avery's First Orgasm.'

Eek! I was hoping he'd forgotten that comment I'd made at the coffee shop, but clearly he hasn't. I clamp my thighs together and remind myself to breathe. There are no words for the tingles Jase can send through my body with only his deep, sexy voice. That certainly never happened with my high school boyfriend, Brent.

'Whistle? You okay?' He takes my hand and absently traces his thumb across my palm. 'Breathe for me, okay.'

I pull in a ragged breath, still unable to speak.

His cocky smile is back. 'Just think about it, babe.'

I manage a nod.

Jase takes a sip from his coffee, his eyes still watching mine over the brim of the cup. 'There's something I don't understand,' he says, running a hand through his messy hair. 'You said you had a high school boyfriend, and you guys were pretty serious...'

Oh God, I can't have him asking questions about Brent. 'Uh huh.'

'And yet, you've never...' He raises his eyebrows. 'So I take it you guys never messed around?'

I feel like I'm having an out of body experience. I can't believe Jase wants to talk about my past...love life, or lack thereof. This is crazy. I feel like I'm floating above us, watching, preparing to witness my demise. 'We experimented a little, but never had sex.'

He frowns. 'And no orgasms for you?'

'Why are you so obsessed with my non-orgasmic status? Some girls just don't have them, okay?'

'Um, no. That is most definitely *not okay* with me.'

I roll my eyes. 'Madison said I probably would have if he... never mind.' I need a muzzle. Seriously, I should be shot. The things he'll get me to admit to....

Jase pins me with an icy glare. 'If he what?'

'Used his mouth,' I squeak out. It wasn't actually how she'd put it, but I wouldn't use those rude words to describe it.

'And he wouldn't?' Jase's eyes widen.

I shake my head. 'He said he didn't do that.'

Jase throws his head back in disgust, groaning as his eyes roll back in his head. 'Any guy who has a policy against that is a fucking idiot.'

The nervous waves crashing inside me erupt into an all-out frenzy with this information. Jase's opinion on oral sex shouldn't ignite my sex-drive, make my skin tingle, or heat my lady parts, yet that's exactly what happens.

His expression grows dark, more serious as he leans in closer. 'Baby, if you let me, I wouldn't come up for a week.'

Holy. Crap.

Chapter 16

Avery

The email sitting in my inbox is taunting me, distracting me in the most wondrous way. It's a follow-up from the adoption agency. It's a simple, three-line email, but the news it contains is about to change my life. They've confirmed that they mailed the information about my birth mother to my dorm address. I even have a tracking number to chart the package's progress if I want.

I shove away from my desk, unable to stare at the words any longer. I need to get dressed anyway, and finish drying my hair. Madison's humming to herself as she applies the rest of her makeup in front of the full-length mirror, completely oblivious to my inner turmoil. Now that the information is on its way, it feels like a ticking time bomb, surely set to explode in my face once it finds me. I suppose I don't have to open it if I don't want to. Who am I kidding? Of course I'll open it. I've waited nineteen years to know this information. No matter what happens, something inside me needs to know.

Mitch never called, not that I care. I'd rather be with Jase anyway. I put my hair up in a ponytail, knowing there will be no taming its crazy tonight, and check my outfit in the mirror. Dark skinny jeans, ballet flats and a simple white silk top, rolled at the elbows. I add a few colorful beaded necklaces and call it good.

'You look pretty.' Madison smiles at my reflection. She has a date tonight, but she's being surprisingly cool and level-headed about me going to the Delta Sig party.

'Thanks. You look smokin'.' Her little purple dress and cowgirl boots couldn't be more adorable. I would totally need to borrow those at some point.

She pulls me in for an unexpected hug. 'Jase better know how great you are. He does anything to mess this up, I'll feed him his balls,' she says, patting my back.

I nod silently. I don't tell her that I'm probably going to be the one to mess things up.

When I reach the house, I'm happy to see Jase was right. It's a low key party compared to their usual bashes. Tonight is close friends only. There are about thirty people there, spread out in the living room and kitchen, mingling and talking against the backdrop of low music. It's a totally different vibe than their usual raging parties. It's nice.

Unfortunately, Stacia is one of the few guests here. She grins at me coyly. I know she hates my friendship with Jase, and I hate her very existence. It's a strange thing that all of that is communicated in a single glance shared between us.

I find Jase in the kitchen, a bottle of beer dangling from his hand, and a cool, easy smile on his lips as he talks to Trey. I take a moment just to admire him across the room. It's nice to see him relaxed like this. His hip is leaning against the counter, his feet crossed at the ankles. His T-shirt is a size too small and hugs his biceps nicely. I let out a contented sigh and saunter toward him.

Jase's eyes find mine and his smile widens. 'Whistle! Get your hot ass over here.' He reaches for me once I'm close and pulls me to his side.

Part of me absolutely loves how close we're becoming. Part of me is terrified by it. Jase doesn't yet know my past, and I have no idea how things will pan out when he does. But when the heavy weight of his arm curls around my waist and pulls me close, all my fears vanish. Standing at his side, I can pretend for just a moment that I belong here, that all is okay. I smile at his dumbass friend Trey, tap my feet to the music and gratefully take the can of soda Jase passes me.

Jase is still watching me, his brilliant blue eyes sparkling. I love the way he looks at me, but it's getting me all flustered. My eyes reluctantly leave his, only to be assaulted by two sorority girls eagerly making out for show. Gah! I can't un-see that. Yes, because I wanted to develop eye-cancer tonight.

'I'll be right back. I'm just gonna run to the bathroom.' All these overdressed girls have me wanting to go check my reflection.

Jase nods and removes his warm arm from my waist.

I round the corner and run smack into Stacia. She staggers back, her eyes unfocused as she takes me in. Great. She's drunk again. If she thinks she's staying the night in Jase's room, she's wrong. Hell, I'll stay there myself just to be sure. The thought makes my stomach flip.

I plant my hands on my hips, mentally preparing for the show-down she's intent we have. 'Excuse me, can I go by?' I say, struggling to keep my voice calm.

She rolls her eyes, pointing a manicured finger in my face. 'You won't last, you know. He'll sleep with you, then move on like he does with all the rest. I'm the only one who sticks around. It's always been that way and always will be.'

I push my shoulders back and fake a confidence I don't feel. 'Back off, Stacia. I'm seeing Jase. Not you.' Wow, that popped out of nowhere, but maybe it's at least partially true.

'Not exclusively,' she returns, batting her eyelashes, leaving me to wonder what the hell she means.

She's rendered me momentarily speechless. Bitter words die on my tongue, and I shove my way around her. Fighting my way into the bathroom, I slump against the door and breathe. A pale, wide-eyed girl stares back at me. God! I hate Stacia. I hate that I let her get to me. I don't know what Jase and I have; I only know I don't want her having any part of it.

I give myself a pep-talk, use the restroom, wash my hands and then attempt to rejoin the party. Only I'm stopped in my tracks again, this time by something a million times worse than facing off with Stacia. My stomach drops to my feet.

Marcy Capri, with the same frizzy blond hair she had in high school, is standing in the hall, deep in conversation with Stacia.

Shit!

I slip around the corner before they spot me, my heart staggering and tripping over itself. Every part of me shakes and my head is a mess. I do the only thing I can think to do. I reach in my pocket, drag out my whistle and blow it as hard as I can.

Chapter 17

Jase

The shrill whistle cuts through the air with an insistent blast.

Avery…

I shove past bodies to follow the sound and find her alone in the hallway. She's slumped against the wall, knees drawn up to her chest…and she's crying. *What the fuck?*

I scoop her up in my arms, carry her to the nearby bathroom and lock the door behind us. I set her on the counter and push her hair back from her face. 'Avery, baby…Tell me what happened.'

She sucks in a shuddering breath, biting her bottom lip. 'I'm sorry I'm such a mess.' She uses the back of her hand to brush the stray tears from her cheeks and looks up at me with a pained expression.

'Whistle? Did someone touch you? Tell me what happened.' My blood is pounding in my veins. If someone hurt her, I will lose it.

She shakes her head. 'No, nothing like that. It's just…I saw someone from my past…remembered things I didn't want to remember…' Little hiccups rack her chest, and tears still swim in her eyes.

If I could take away whatever she's been through, I'd do it. I hate how powerless I feel. 'Avery, tell me who he is. Let me handle this.'

She swallows down a sob. 'Not he. She. And please don't do anything, it'll make things worse.'

She?

Fuck. I hate her past; I hate whatever this is that won't let her move forward. 'Avery, talk to me.'

'Not about this, please, Jase. Don't make me. Can we just pretend…for one more night…please?'

The look in her eyes is breaking my fucking heart. 'Tell me what you need. I'll do it, Whistle, please. Tell me.'

She shakes her head. 'I can't tell you, Jase. I don't know how.'

Using two fingers, I tip her chin up. 'Then let me make you forget whoever did this to you. Let me help you.'

She nods slowly, her green eyes searing mine with their intensity. 'Please…'

She doesn't say another word, because my lips crash against hers, but a low moan breaks in her throat. This is the only way I know how to help her, and it seems she's okay with letting me try.

My fingers find the button on her jeans, my tongue still stroking hers. Despite her fears and warnings about going slow, we both know we've been building towards this the entire time. It's the only weapon in my arsenal to drive her past away. And I will use it. I know of no other way to bring her relief. Operation Avery's First Orgasm is a Go.

Avery

My jeans and panties are at my knees, constricting my movements, but my limited mobility doesn't hamper Jase any. His fingers find the spot my body needs him most, stroking, rubbing, stopping briefly to wet his fingers with his mouth, then caressing me again. The way his slick fingers slide across my sensitive flesh makes me cry out. He lifts my shirt and pulls down the cups of my bra so I'm exposed, kissing and suckling each of my breasts, his mouth and tongue constantly exploring, keeping rhythm with his fingers that are sending me closer and closer to the edge.

His wet kisses move to my throat, and I shamelessly rock my hips against his hand, needing more. Reading my body, he pushes one finger inside me and lets out a groan of his own when he penetrates me. He knows my body better than I do and he gives me what I need before I even have to ask. A girl could get used to this kind of treatment.

I'm about to come undone, and Jase is taking me there. I lock my knees, my hands scrambling for something to hold onto just as I'm almost there. Suddenly Jase removes his hand and plants a chaste kiss on my lips. *Is he stopping?*

'Jase, don't stop. I think I can come…'

He looks at me with a devilish smirk. 'Oh, I know you can, baby. But the guys can hear you, and I have a feeling you're going to be even louder when I make you come. Let's go to my room.'

Crap! They were listening? I realize the party that was in full swing when we started this has gone eerily quiet.

He slides my panties and jeans into place, zipping and buttoning them for me, while I stand there uselessly, trying and failing to calm my frantic heart.

'When we go out there, just ignore them. Okay?' He drops another kiss on my mouth and I merely nod.

I'm not sure how long we were tucked away in the bathroom – at least twenty minutes, I think. Jase takes my hand and exits first. The hallway is clear, but when we pass by the living room cheers erupt – applause, whistling, hoots and hollers. My cheeks flame like never before. God, this is embarrassing. I tuck my chin to my chest, not daring to meet their eyes, and follow Jase to the staircase. We jog up all three flights to the attic and are breathless once we reach his room.

Turning on the soft lamp on his dresser, Jase shuts and locks the door, then turns to face me. I'm sure my cheeks are still flushed, but he doesn't seem to mind my awkwardness. He stalks toward me like a predator casing its prey, grasping my hips to guide me backwards to his bed.

The things he did to my body, the responses he elicited, I know it's no use pretending I don't want this. Every fear has been silenced; every thought is tangled up with Jase. In this moment, I feel like I could let my past slip away, like I could start fresh with Jase and forget all about Brent and the mistake that shall not be named. This could be my last chance. Stacia could be learning about my past right now.

'Just give me one chance to show you how good we could be together,' he whispers.

The seductive tone of his deep voice and the promise of more breaks all my self-preservation. 'Yes.'

Jase doesn't hesitate, and gives my shoulders a playful shove, so I fall back onto his bed, sitting on the edge. Jase lifts my shirt over my head, and with a quick flick of his wrist, my bra drops open too. I let it fall down my arms and toss it to the floor.

Jase's intense gaze is locked on mine. His lips are parted and slightly swollen from kissing. 'God, you're beautiful.' He drags his knuckles softly across my throat, tracing my collarbone. As if trying to read what I'm ready for, or more importantly what I'm *not* ready for, Jase remains fully-clothed, but helps me remove my jeans. We lie together on his bed, legs tangled together, as close as two bodies can be. I can feel each pounding heartbeat, each breath against my neck. Needing some sort of coverage, I insist my panties stay on, but Jase works around them. He begins exploring my body again, lightly rubbing my arms, trailing kisses down my chest and stomach, and when he settles between my legs and glances up to gauge my reaction, I merely watch him and wait to see what will happen next. There is no willpower in me to stop him.

He pushes my panties to the side and plants an open-mouth kiss *there*. Holy Toledo, the sensation is like nothing else. Jase's warm, wet mouth sends my hips shooting off of the mattress. His tongue slides against me again, and I come undone, bunching the comforter in my fists and calling out his name. The pressure intensifies and then waves of pleasure crash through me. The feeling is more than I ever expected. I will need to do that again. Often.

Jase holds me after, and continues lightly stroking his fingertips down the length of my bare arms as aftershocks make my muscles tremble. My emotions tangle inside me. I feel pure bliss in this moment, happy and safe with him. Then I'm struck by a wave of guilt, because as nice as all this, I know it's been built on a lie.

A few seconds later, Jase returns to kissing me, his hips pressing insistently into mine. His entire body is hard and ready. I run a hand through his hair, like I've wanted to do since the first night I saw him. Dropping one more light kiss against my mouth, Jase leans back just slightly to watch me. My breathing is finally returning to normal, though my heart is still pounding.

'That feel good, babe?' he asks.

'Amazing. Thank you.'

His smile grows. He's clearly proud of himself over my loud and very unladylike orgasm. 'Anytime.'

'I'm sorry I can't…return the favor.'

'It's okay,' his voice is thick. 'That's not why I did it. You don't have to do anything you don't want to do.'

'It's not that…it's just, I'll gag.'

'Hmm.' He stokes my cheek. 'We'll work up to it.'

'Is it really that important?'

'It's kind of my favorite.' His lips curve in a soft smile.

Oh brother…

Chapter 18

Jase

I offer Avery one of my T-shirts, and she quietly slips it on over her head, then curls against my pillow in an unspoken agreement that she's staying the night. Seeing her lying in my bed, swallowed up in my shirt is the best sight ever. Knowing she's sleeping in my arms tonight, that she's sharing parts of herself with me despite her fears, does heady things to my protective instincts. I still wish I knew what was going on inside that pretty head of hers, but I know we'll get there. Tonight was a big step forward. And I won't soon forget the way she tastes, the sultry sound of her raspy gasps calling my name. Fuck, that was hot.

I turn off the light and join her in the bed, spooning up against her back so I can fold her into my arms. Her hair smells like strawberries and I lean in to kiss the back of her neck. 'Just rest. Everything's going to be okay,' I mumble against her skin.

She lets out a soft sigh and relaxes against me.

I don't know what set her off tonight, but I'm happy that she came to me for comfort. I'll never forget the feeling of panic when I heard that whistle cut through the party. I didn't even realize she carried it with her; I'd sort of gotten it as a joke. But part of me loved knowing she kept it with her, and used it to call me when she needed me.

In the morning, we sleep late, and grab coffee and muffins on campus before I drive her to her dorm. I wouldn't mind spending the day with her just lounging in my bed, but she says she has homework, so I reluctantly let her go.

At the curb outside her building, I hold her tightly to my chest and kiss her.

'Thanks for everything last night,' she says, blinking up at me.

'Anytime.' I kiss her once more and let her go. 'Better go write that journaling assignment on orgasms now…' I grin.

She takes a step away and stumbles on the sidewalk, but I catch her elbow before she goes down. Heat blossoms in her cheeks and she shoots me a glare.

'Call me later, babe.'

She nods once, then flees into her dorm.

Chapter 19

Jase

I clean my room twice, even maneuvering the clunky vacuum up three flights of stairs, because I can't remember the last time I actually used it, which means I'm probably due.

By the time I'm done, there are vacuum lines on the rug beside my bed, and the room smells like citrus furniture polish.

I can't ever remember feeling this way about a girl before – it's kind of intense. Avery and I are opposites in every way, yet still I love being around her. But maybe that's why we work well together – I'm outgoing and she's closed off; I've lived and taken chances where she's been guarded; I pull her out of her shell and she keeps me sane. She gets my sense of humor; she hit it off with my mom, and last night... Fuck. Last night is in a category all its own. Watching her come undone like that. Shit, that was hot. Tasting her, hearing her breathy moans, I'm half hard just thinking about it. Avery arouses so many emotions in me. I want to protect her, make her smile, and take care of her every need.

It's a far cry from how I ever was with Stacia. I hate to say it, but I put myself before her needs pretty much every time. With Avery, putting her first is what I want. It's weird.

I finish cleaning my room, lug the vacuum cleaner back downstairs and stash it in a closet that contains a half-inflated blow up doll and a collection of sports equipment. Then I jump in the shower. I want to be fresh for Avery. I even shave and take a little time on manscaping, making sure things are presentable in case she wants to venture south. It's probably hopeful thinking on my part. But I want it to be her idea to go there. And I pray that she does, because as awesome as last night was, it was fucking hard. Literally. I barely constrained the urge to go jerk off while she was getting ready for bed. But I won't pressure her. Clearly this is all new for her, and even though I don't know much about her past yet, I know her jackass ex-boyfriend did something to make her cautious.

When Avery arrives I've just come back upstairs with popcorn and two cans of soda.

'Hey.' She smiles at me from the doorway, watching me inside my room.

'Hey.' I set down the snacks and turn to face her. She makes a pair of jeans and a gray T-shirt look sexy. And her hair is just the way I like it – tumbling loose around her shoulders. 'Come here.'

I open my arms and Avery crosses the room, letting herself be pulled in against me. She rests her head against my chest and sighs contentedly. I wonder if I didn't initiate the physical contact between us if she would, but I doubt it. My girl is as timid as they come. I hate whoever made her this way. I want her to tell me, to open up, but I trust that she will in time.

'You get to choose the movie,' I tell her, taking a step back to release her.

She nods and peruses the collection of DVDs I've rounded up from the guys in the house. Most are comedies with dirty humor or horror flicks, but she doesn't complain. She selects a paranormal thriller and hands it to me.

'Are you sure?'

She nods. 'I love scary movies.'

'Really?' I'm not sure why, but this surprises me. Maybe because she's so sweet and innocent. Either way, I love that she's into it. I've wanted to see this movie for a while. 'Well, if you get too scared and need to sleep over, you're welcome to.' *Smooth, Jase.*

She grins crookedly. 'Like a slumber party?'

'Ah no, not like a slumber party. Like me and you in my bed spooning and hopefully kissing.'

Her cheeks blush pink and she tips her head down. I can't resist tipping her chin up with two fingers. I press a soft kiss to her mouth and then look at her to gauge her reaction. 'Are you okay with what happened last night? I mean…you liked it, right?'

'I thought that was obvious, yes.'

I dare a step closer. 'So maybe this whole tutoring thing can be extended a bit…'

Avery bites her bottom lip. 'Extended how?'

'Hmm…' I place a hand on her waist, drawing her closer. 'Let me show you.'

Thirty minutes later, the movie plays on my laptop, all but forgotten, and Avery is lying in my arms, resting her head in my favorite spot − in the center of my chest. Trailing my fingers lightly across her arms, I never want her to move from this spot. She fits perfectly tucked against me and her hair smells so good.

All too soon, Avery lifts her head to look up at me with sad eyes I wish were happy.

'Everything okay?' I ask. 'Movie's not too scary for you, is it?'

It's more a psychological thriller than blood-and-gore, but she looks like something's bothering her. I get the sense there's something more on her mind than movies and cuddling. There's a little crease in between her eyebrows and she drags her teeth across her bottom lip.

'It's…never mind.' She drops her head to my chest, nestling herself in once again.

I'm torn on whether or not to let it go, but there's a nagging feeling inside me. I roll us over on the bed so I'm hovering over top of her. Her eyes widen in surprise as our aligned bodies command her attention. I smooth her hair back from her face, tucking it behind her ears. 'Hey, you know you can talk to me, right?'

She nods. 'I'm not ready yet. I don't want things to end between us.'

My thumb lingers on her cheek. I want to tell her she's wrong, that she's safe and this isn't going to end, but something gives me pause and instead I nod. 'Okay.'

I lean in and kiss her, soft at first, but after a few moments our kisses turn deeper and her legs wind themselves around my back, and I'm reminded of how long it's been since I was with anyone. Not good. I force a deep breath into my lungs and let it out slowly, focusing on slowing our pace, even as Avery's tongue flirts relentlessly with mine. A small frustrated groan escapes her throat as she tightens her legs around my waist, forcing her pelvis to rub against mine. I give in and grind back against her, my body reacting to the friction. *Shiiit. She feels too good.*

Several minutes later I break away, breathless with desire and her sleepy eyes meet mine at the sudden halt in action. 'Avery…if you're not sure about going further, I'm going to need to stop.' I wish I could phrase it a more graceful way, but fuck, she's gonna make me come.

I can tell she's conflicted – her body wants this, but her head isn't so sure. 'Hey, it's okay. I just…haven't been with anyone in a while and a certain part of my body likes you rubbing against up against him.'

She smiles with understanding. 'I know. My body likes you too. A lot.'

What is she telling me? Does she want to go farther? 'Avery?'

She swallows, summoning her courage. 'I hate that I have to think about this. I want this. I do. I just…'

'Shh.' I silence her with a quick kiss. She's thinking way too hard. 'You had fun last night, right?'

A silly grin curves her mouth upward. 'What gave you that idea?'

I kiss her again. 'Hm. It might have tipped me off when you were screaming my name…'

Her cheeks flush. 'Jase…'

'Yeah, baby?'

She's stewing, working her bottom lip in between her teeth. 'I wish I could just let go, be with you like I want to.'

I think I understand what she's saying. She hates how her wounded past makes her cautious. I get it. I do. There are certain events in life that change a person. Like with my mom. I'll probably never be that same carefree guy again. I'll be more watchful, more aware that everything can be taken away when you least expect it. I just wish I could make things easier for her. 'Let me take care of you. No thinking tonight. Be with me like you want to. Let me make you feel good.'

She nods. 'Yes.'

I lean toward her and drop a soft kiss against her mouth, her throat, the curve of collarbone. Taking my time, I remove each piece of her clothing, kissing her exposed skin as I go, but leaving her panties in place. That will have to be her decision to make. I pull my shirt off over my head, needing to feel her warm skin against mine. I kiss each breast, rub against the damp barrier her panties provide until she's moaning my name. Reading her body, I push the fabric aside and give her the contact she needs. Her knees fall apart and she whimpers loudly, rolling her hips. Watching Avery come is fucking hot. Suddenly I'm harder than I've ever been, but then Avery's reaching her warm hand into my boxers and stroking me. Faster than I would have thought possible, I lose it. I curl my hand around hers to shield her from the mess that empties from me.

'Fuck, Avery.' I breathe, planting a kiss against her temple.

She smiles, content and clearly pleased with herself over making me come.

I grab some tissues from beside my bed and clean us both off, then lie back beside her. 'Stay the night with me?' I ask.

'Yes.' Her eyes blaze with confidence and certainty.

I get the feeling she's saying yes to more than just a sleepover. She's saying yes to me, to life, and I pull her against me and hold her tight.

Chapter 20

Avery

I'm still smiling like an idiot as I make it to my dorm room. Madison's sitting on the futon painting her nails when I arrive. She studies my wrinkled clothes and messy sleep-styled hair with a smirk. 'Have fun last night?'

'Yes.' I bite my cheek to avoid squeeing. 'It was fun. How was your date?'

'Dull.' She shrugs. 'Oh, a package came for you.' Madison nods toward the desk where a large envelope awaits.

Wow. It's here. A flash of warmth invades my chest.

Madison pauses, holding the bottle of polish. 'Avery? What is it?'

'Hm?' I pluck the envelope. 'It's probably just nothing.' *Lie.* This envelope is everything: The cure to my identity crisis, a link to my past, and a possible future with my mom. Tears prick my eyes, and still clutching the envelope, I head off for the communal bathrooms, needing a moment to myself.

I pull open the curtain to the shower on the far end and sit on the cool tiled bench seat.

Then I hesitate. Maybe I shouldn't be alone when I open it. I dial Jase's number, but the call goes to voicemail. After waiting several minutes, I send him a text. I balance the phone on the bench seat beside me. Since he usually replies right away, I'm surprised when he doesn't text me back.

I've been waiting a lifetime for this moment, and I'm unable to put it off for even another second. I tear open the envelope and slide out the inch thick stack of papers.

I know Jase said he didn't have any plans today, so I'm wondering where he could be. That question settles like an uneasy pit in my stomach, but I push it to the back of my mind as I begin reading the opening letter, addressed to me, on the adoption agency letter-head. It acknowledges the difficult journey this process may prove to be and lists resources to help deal with birthparent searches. Awesome. Even they don't have faith in their process.

The following pages contain boring forms and information that my dads had to complete nineteen years ago. It's funny to see that their handwriting hasn't changed a bit in all that time. Seeing the sheer volume of forms and information they supplied overwhelms me. They must've really wanted me bad. That thought makes me smile, though it's quickly followed by a pang of guilt about doing this behind their backs.

I continue leafing through the pages, knowing the good stuff is probably at the back of the pile.

Bingo.

An old photograph of a woman that looks shockingly familiar is clipped to the back page. The same wavy auburn hair and wide-set eyes that greet me in the mirror each morning are staring back at me. I pull in a deep breath, shocked by how young she looks.

Her first name and a generic email account are supplied on the last page.

Huh.

Jessica.

My mom's name is Jessica.

I'm strangely devoid of emotion as I learn this. Her photo is captivating, though, and I find myself staring at it, brushing it lovingly with my thumb. Tears sting my eyes, and as scary as it is, I stuff the papers back into the envelope and head back to my room to email her. Lord help me for whatever happens next.

I haven't heard from Jase in two days. I've called and texted several times, and still nothing. I'm more worried than anything else, and since he didn't show up for class today either, I head straight to his house after.

I let myself in when no one answers the front door. Geez, they should probably keep it locked. The house is empty and quiet, and although my heart is pounding at what I might find, I climb the stairs to the attic. There could be a million reasons for him not calling me back...he could have the flu, maybe something happened with his mom...or the worst – is he back with Stacia? Yet, even as I try to justify his silence, I know it can only mean one thing. I saw Marcy and Stacia talking the other night. I'm sure they saw me too. I guess I just hoped maybe Jase wouldn't have to find out this way – and from Stacia of all people.

Steeling myself for the worst, I knock on Jase's door. A few seconds later, I hear the floorboards creak as he crosses the room. A ragged looking Jase peers back at me. He isn't dressed, hasn't shaved and his hair's a complete wreck.

'Jase?'

He doesn't say anything for several seconds, just continues watching me with guarded eyes. The pain I see reflected back at me is too much. This is why I don't get close to people. This look. I hate being responsible for it when they learn I'm not who they want me to be.

'Can I come in? Explain at least?' I ask.

Jase's brow is wrinkled in confusion, but he opens the door a few more inches and saunters away. It's not exactly a warm welcome, but he's not shutting me out just yet, either. I step through the door and pull in a steadying breath. I've never wanted to explain this before. When confronted with my past, I always flee. Always. But Jase deserves more. So as much as it's going to suck to tell him this story, I know I have to.

His room is cold and any and all warmth between us is absent too. Jase turns to face me. 'Did you know about the pictures?' he asks.

I swallow the grapefruit-sized lump that's lodged itself painfully in my throat. That's the thing – it'd be easier to say no, that Brent had tricked me, I didn't know I was being photographed. But I did know. Brent thought it would be fun, sexy. And I would have done just about anything to hear him say he loved me. It turns out when you have abandonment issues, you'll do just about anything to feel loved. I needed to feel loved, to be close to someone, and I loved it when Brent held me or touched me. Whether or not it had anything to do with my adoption, I didn't know, but I craved that affection. During those moments of feeling wanted and desired, it dampened my sense of abandonment. I know these are probably all excuses, and certainly not something Jase is likely to understand. Nor does it erase the fact I kept it from him.

I hang my head, not wanting to see his eyes when I tell him this next part. 'Yeah, I knew.' I didn't say yes to the idea right away – he wore me down over a couple of weeks. And of course what followed wasn't heartfelt; it wasn't filled with love at all. It was an experience that left me broken, shattered, and humiliated. 'When we broke up a couple weeks later, he shared the images with his friends, which were quickly passed around our school.' I could barely get out of bed those first few days. My dads thought I had the flu.

116

The disappointment in Jase's eyes is so severe, so all encompassing, I stagger a step back, struggling to remain on my feet. It's the look I hoped I never had to see it cross his face.

Some of the photos, Brent and I had taken together, a few I took of myself and texted to him while we were dating. 'I didn't know how to bring it up,' I say.

'You have a fucking sex tape, Avery!' He throws his hands up in the air. 'These are things you mention.' He punches the wall. 'Goddamn it!'

His fist leaves a dent in the drywall, and I stifle the urge to go to him and inspect his hand. I figured it was only a matter of time before Jase found out, but I never imagined he'd actually see it. Of course, Marcy probably pulled it up on her phone.

My stomach cramps and I think I might actually be sick.

'Do your dads know?' Jase's voice is low and controlled, like he's barely holding back his anger.

'Of course not. They'd shit a brick.'

'Yeah, imagine how I feel.'

I meet his eyes. 'How do you feel?' Even if his next words crush me, I need to know.

'I was falling for you, Avery.'

All the oxygen leaves the room. 'Was?'

'Was. Am. Fuck I don't know.' His voice is raspy and weak, slashing away at my heart. His hands tear angrily through his hair, leaving it standing on end.

Something vital for my survival has been ripped from my body. Something I didn't even know I had, and now can't fathom living without.

I tuck my chin to my chest. 'It wasn't a sex tape.'

Brent and his best friend had created a slideshow of all the images both he and I had taken. The end product looped like a video, lasting several minutes.

'Close enough. There were parts of you that I've never even seen exposed for the whole world to appreciate.' The vacant quality of his voice, the hurt in his eyes is so real, I feel it in the pit of my stomach.

'I'm sorry…I'm sorry I ever took those pictures. I'm sorry I didn't tell you…'

'Me too. You're not who I thought you were,' he says simply.

I hate the dejected tone of his voice. Seething anger, screaming, yelling would be better than this defeated tone.

'Don't you think I wish I could take this back? I would if I could,' I whisper.

His eyes flick up to mine, devoid of all the warmth I used to feel from those beautiful baby blues. 'I wish you could, too.' He turns his back and the tension in his shoulders tells me our conversation is done. And worse. We are done too.

Chapter 21

Jase

'Stacia, quit!' I chuckle, unable to stop myself, because it turns out after about ten beers, the tight feeling in my chest becomes numb. And my equally drunk ex-girlfriend is a distraction I can't seem to turn down. She's on the couch next to me, trying to tickle me. I forgot how grabby she gets after a few drinks.

Stacia removes her hands from under my shirt and bites her lip. The practiced look of seduction on her face is familiar and comforting. It would be so easy to fall back into things with her, even if it's not what I really want. But my brain is tired of trying to work through what I had with Avery, and how I feel now. I wish I could un-see those images and go back to not knowing, but that's not possible. At first I was pissed at Stacia for thrusting that girl's phone in my face and showing me my innocent, sweet Avery being anything but sweet, or innocent. But after I got done cursing and punched the wall a couple of times, I knew Stacia wasn't the one I was mad at.

The party around us has died down significantly, and there are just a few of us left – the guys that live here and their hookups. I know Stacia is waiting patiently tonight to see if she'll have a shot with me, and honestly, I don't know. I haven't even decided yet. Which probably means my dick will decide for me later. And since he's easily fooled by Stacia, I have a feeling I know what'll happen.

Avery and I were never official, and after the way her past was thrown into my face like that… I don't owe her anything. She left the other day without saying anything else, though what could she say after I saw numerous pictures of her with another guy's junk in her mouth? God, I hate that this side of her even existed. The urge to hit something again spikes inside me, just as Stacia leans closer.

'Take me upstairs,' she whispers.

I push the images from my head and curl my fingers around Stacia's, needing something warm and familiar to grasp onto. 'Come on.'

I lie in bed, waiting for Stacia to return from the bathroom, wondering what the fuck I'm doing. When she appears in the doorway and saunters toward my bed, I curse the lamp on my dresser currently lighting the room. This would be easier if I didn't have to look at her, because my mind won't stop comparing her to Avery. Avery's soft auburn hair, those wide green eyes.

When Stacia straddles my lap, I let my eyes slip closed. And when she leans down to kiss me, I fight to turn off my brain. Yet it's impossible not to notice that her mouth doesn't fit against mine like Avery's, that she smells different, that she wears too much perfume.

'Wait.' I break the kiss and Stacia opens her eyes. 'Go turn off the lights.'

She frowns. 'You never used to want the lights off.'

'I know, but I do now.'

She bites her cheek, her mind working, but she dutifully climbs from my lap and crosses the room to switch off the lamp. Once the room is lit by just the dim moonlight, she saunters back toward me, removing her shirt and bra before she reaches the bed. The familiarity of her should comfort me, but my mind is reeling.

She rubs a manicured hand against my uninterested cock. 'Just relax, Jase. Let me take care of this tonight.'

I don't want her. But would it be so bad to do this? To let her try and make me forget the girl I really wanted? Stacia knows we aren't together. We've been down this road before. It won't change anything between us. Stacia's fingers fumble with my belt buckle and I close my eyes again, fighting to make myself relax.

Chapter 22

Avery

I hate how alone I feel without Jase. We haven't spoken since that heated exchange in his room after he found out about my past. I know I shouldn't have, but a tiny piece of me was hoping that he'd be okay with it. Well, not *okay*, but maybe more understanding. I guess he isn't who I thought he was, either. It was stupid to think he could be the one to save me. I'd learned long ago to rely on myself and not put too much stock in others. They just let me down in the end anyway.

I can't change my past. And as much as I wish I could, I can't track down every person who downloaded that degrading photo collage. The only thing I can control is what I do next.

Realizing it's time to deal with my identity issues and face my past once and for all, I open my laptop and log into my email account. I debate over creating a generic email address that can't be linked to me, but in the end, I want my birthmom to know my name, to know who I am.

I type what I had intended to be a brief message, but it turns out when you're emailing your mom for the first time, there's a lot to say. I tell her about my dads, how I had a great childhood, and that I am in college now. I tell her about my roommate and our crazy gay friend, Noah, who likes to borrow our clothes. I spill my heart out in my note, hoping she'll laugh when she reads it and understand that I am a normal, happy girl. Or heck, maybe I'm just trying to prove to myself that I really am; either way, I hit send before I change my mind and delete it all.

Madison returns from class a short time later, dropping her bag to the floor and turning to face me with a concerned expression. 'Hey…How are you?' The sympathy in her eyes is new.

'Um, fine I guess.'

She crosses the room and hugs me, pulling me firmly into her arms. *Uh-oh*. Madison is not a hugger.

'What's wrong?' I ask, wrapping one arm awkwardly around her back.

'We need to talk.' She pulls back suddenly, her hands resting against my shoulders. 'Jase stopped me after class today.'

Oh.

Crap.

'And?'

'And he told me. Everything.'

My heart sinks.

Madison continues, 'At first he was coy, asking me about your dating background, your experience with guys.' She let out a nervous chuckle. 'I basically told him you wouldn't know what to do if a cock slapped you upside the head. But he informed me I was wrong. At first, I was proud, but then he explained about the pictures your ex used to exploit you, and I'm so sorry, Avery, I had no idea. Now I feel terrible that I always tried to get you to break out of your shell. I thought you were just a little shy – not scarred from a traumatic event.'

'It's okay, Madison. I just don't really tell people about it. But I am okay.'

'Really?' Her brow wrinkles in concern.

I shrug. 'I'm trying to deal. It's not like I have a choice. And I don't want to hide under a rock anymore.'

Her smile grows, pushing her mouth upwards. 'Good, hun. That's good.' She gives my hand a squeeze 'I'm here for you.'

'Thanks, Mads.' I shouldn't care, but I do, and I can't resist probing for information on Jase. 'So what was Jase's mood like?'

Madison's smile falls. 'He seemed sad, worried about you, but mostly sad. He wanted to make sure you're okay.'

'Oh.' I don't know what this means, or how to process this information. It isn't like he calls me anymore, or even sits near me in our shared class. I can't control Jase's response to learning about my past. The only things I can do is move forward, and pray that everything works out like it's supposed to.

Chapter 23

Jase

Removing Stacia from my bed and my life again is a bigger pain in the ass than I was expecting. We're not dating and we're not together, but she seems to have blocked out that information. Ever since the drunken night where we messed around and passed out in my bed, she's been coming over every day. Today, I've got to put an end to that. Even if I wasn't still plagued by memories of Avery, I know I don't want Stacia.

When Stacia arrives, I make sure I'm waiting for her downstairs. I don't want her getting cozy up in my room.

She's all smiles when she comes in and tosses her purse on the couch.

'We need to talk,' I say.

Her face falls and she tenses up.

She can tell by my stiff posture things aren't going to go her way. 'Sorry Stacia, I'm just not feeling it,' I mutter, rubbing a hand over the back of my neck.

'You seemed to be *feeling it* just fine when you were in my mouth last weekend.'

Christ.

She snatches the purse she's just deposited on the couch. 'You know what, Jase? Don't waste your breath. I'm done with your shit.'

'I'm sorry, okay?'

She rolls her eyes and stomps to the door, which I pull open for her. 'I've been sleeping with Trey anyway,' she adds before slamming the door in my face.

Nice.

I turn the lock on the door as if to prove a point. Stacia is done invading my life. That chapter is closed. As for Avery...I'm not sure yet.

Chapter 24

Avery

'Enough moping,' Madison says, snatching the dirty romance novel from my hands. 'Come on, you're coming out with me and Noah.'

'But I was at the part where he spanks her for the first time…' Wow. I can't believe I just said that. I also can't believe I'm reading the book that Madison shoved into my hands after finishing it in one day. But she's right, it is addicting.

'Told ya you'd love the smut. But you can read it later. We're going bowling.'

I don't want to give up the progress I've made, so I get dressed, add makeup and let Madison straighten my long, crazy hair. The girl in the mirror looks different, but she's still me. Maybe even a better version of me. No longer terrified of being discovered, because the worst of that has happened – a guy I was falling for found out in the most spectacular fashion and hasn't spoken to me since – and it can't get much worse than that. So I'm done hiding in the dorms while my friends go out on the weekends. Maybe if I pretend I'm normal and not destroyed by Jase' rejection, things will fall into place. Fake it till you make it. Right?

With the truth out in the world, I should feel freer. But the effect is more like a great burden. It's no longer necessary to hide. I feel worse than ever. I should've had the guts to tell Jase. He was a big part of my healing, and he opened himself up a lot along the way, too. By keeping it from him, I cheapened the entire experience. If he is done with me, I at least want to keep our memories, but now they are soured with my own guilt and self-loathing.

When we reach the bowling alley, all promises of a low key evening go up in smoke. Delta Sig has rented out half the place for a private party. *You have got to be kidding me.* I pause at the entrance and Madison looks past me to the group of obnoxiously drunk guys taking up half the bowling alley.

'Did you know?' I turn to her.

'No. I swear. We can go somewhere different if you want.'

Noah takes my hand and gives it a squeeze. 'You're not running away this time, love. You got this.'

I nod. 'Yeah. Okay.' I think I can do this.

Noah pays for our lane while Madison and I go get fitted for our hideous bowling shoes. Madison leads the way back to our lane, which is thankfully on the opposite side from the Delta Sig guys. I don't see Jase. It's possible he's not here. But either way, I know I won't be able to relax with the promise of his presence looming in the background.

Seeing him in the flesh would force up feelings I can't manage right now. I thought I was healing, but his presence assures me that was not the case. Far from it. I miss his hugs that lifted me clear off the floor, his stupid nickname for me, the sexy gleam in his eye when he wanted to kiss me…

I select a ball and when I turn, I spot Jase and Stacia across the room. *Ugh. As if seeing him isn't bad enough…* Stacia wraps her arms around his waist and, even though his hands remain loose at his sides, he does nothing to stop her roaming hands from mauling him. The pain of watching them together stabs at my chest. Maybe I'd overestimated everything we'd shared. Perhaps he and Stacia have always been more than just friendly exes and I refused to see it. Just as Stacia pointed out to me once before, he and I were never exclusive. That doesn't mean the ache of losing him hurts any less. Especially the way it went down. The icy look in his eyes, the flat tone of his voice – I'll never forget that.

Jase leans down and whispers something in Stacia's ear and she bursts out laughing, swatting his arm. Watching this doesn't help my heartache any.

I set the bowling ball down before I drop it on my foot, then I turn to Madison and Noah. 'I was wrong. I need to go.' I have to get out of here before I do something awkward, like start crying in the middle of the bowling alley. Lord, this is ridiculous.

They exchange a glance and nod in silent understanding.

'Yeah, let's go,' Noah agrees. 'These shoes are a total travesty with these slacks.' He makes a point of looking down at the multi-colored shoes and bright red skinny jeans in disgust.

I smile at his half-hearted attempt to make me laugh. I link my arm with Madison's and tuck my chin to my chest, hoping that Jase won't spot me fleeing into the night.

I am done with lying. So when I call my dads requesting they drive my car up to campus, I could tell them I'd changed my mind about wanting my car with me, or that I got a part time job off campus, like I'd talked about doing. But instead, I make them both get on speaker phone and I tell them the truth. I've been in contact with my birthmom through email and am planning to go and meet her in Denver during our upcoming school break.

Their silence is the longest ten seconds of my life. They ultimately agree, saying they knew I'd want to do this eventually, that it's only natural to wonder about where you came from. Humans are wired to want to understand their identity and lineage. They don't like the idea of me going alone, so it takes some convincing, but eventually they come around. I'm not quite sure they are completely onboard with the idea, because they worry about me being disappointed, or hurt, and not to mention driving halfway across the country by myself. But I insist and they relent.

They drive into town on Sunday to drop off my reliable little red sedan, briefly meet Madison and Noah, take me out to lunch and spend the afternoon plotting out my route, covering safety basics on the road, and make me promise to call every day.

They've been way cooler than I ever imagined which makes me feel worse that I considered lying to them. I wonder if they would react so well if I'd kept this from them, and they found out later, from someone other than me. No, I know they'd be livid if that was the case. I can't help but see the similarity about how Jase had found out about my past. I try to tell myself it doesn't matter, and his reaction told me everything. I wonder if things would be different if I'd just told him myself from the beginning. It's too late now. Jase has cast me away like some diseased whore. I am damaged goods in his eyes, and I shouldn't be pining over a guy who doesn't want me. Of course, I wish it was that simple. My body still remembers his touch, and my heart still aches over what has been so cruelly ripped from me.

My computer pings with a new email, and for a brief little second I wonder if it is from Jase. Crossing the room, I stare at my computer screen in disbelief.

Brent?

Why is he contacting me? He went away to school in Florida on a basketball scholarship. At one time, I thought it would suck going to college in two different states. Now, an entire ocean isn't far enough.

I click on the message.

Hey Avery,
You'll probably delete this without reading it. I know I don't deserve the chance to explain, but I've been thinking about everything lately and I wanted to apologize. I did care for you, and I never meant for things to get out like that. I showed a couple guys from the team your sexy photos and, before I knew it, they were everywhere. For what it's worth, I am sorry. I know your senior year sucked after that. You're probably over it, but I wanted you to know.
Brent

I hate that I've been carrying around so much hurt and anger for two years. I hate that I've allowed him to rob me of any time. It sounds rather stupid now that I think about it. I delete the message without responding, deciding I'm done wasting my time on asshats like Brent. I'm over wasting any of my time worrying about crap I can't change. Straightening my shoulders, a slow smile curls on my lips. This is a whole new Avery. I am woman, hear me roar!

Chapter 25

Jase

I drag the phone away from my ear at the shrill of laughter. It's great hearing my mom so chipper, but no one needs this much information on the latest romance novel her book club is reading, least of all her son. *Gah…*

My dad has returned from China and we even manage to exchange a few friendly words over the phone before he hands it over to my mom. To my surprise, he thanks me for coming home to check on her while he was away. I didn't think he'd notice or care, so it's good to know he did.

'How's Avery?' Mom asks next. 'I told your dad how pretty and sweet she is.'

Shit. Just hearing her name is like a kick to the gut. I try to decide what to say next. 'Ah…She and I aren't seeing each other anymore.'

'Jase Alexander Owens. What did you do to screw things up?'

'Nice, Mom. Thanks for automatically assuming it was me.'

She's quiet for a second, but I can tell she won't just let this drop, like I'm silently begging her to do. 'That girl was sweet as pie, Jase, and I could tell how you two felt about each other. What happened?'

I take a deep breath, trying to calm my rioting nerves. 'Let's just say, she was hiding some major skeletons in her closet and she wasn't who I thought she was.' It sounds like a bullshit excuse when I say it out loud. I don't know if I'm hurt because Avery didn't trust me with the truth after I'd been so open with her, or if I'm just hurt that I wasn't the first to be with her.

'Jase, we all have things in our pasts we wish we could take back. You, me, and I know your dad regrets how he handled things with you. But we don't just cut people out of our lives when they make mistakes. I thank God every day that you forgave me. And heaven knows, over the years, you've made your fair share of mistakes, too.'

Shit fuck. I can't argue. 'I guess it was more *how* I found out. I wish Avery would have trusted me enough to come to me herself with the story.'

'Yes, I get it. But did you ask her why she didn't come to you? Give her a chance to explain herself? Maybe she was going to tell you, or maybe she had a good reason why she thought she couldn't.'

Dammit. I hate it when my mom's right.

Her voice softens. 'Just have one more conversation with her, Jase. That's one of my biggest regrets – I wish I would have talked more openly about things with you and your dad. I just don't want you to have any regrets.'

'I love you, Mom.' *Now drop it.*

'Love you more, Jasey. So, are you going to talk to her?'

'We'll see.' After how I treated her, I don't know if Avery will still want to talk to me. And then there's the matter of admitting to her that I fucked up that one night by letting Stacia into my bed. I doubt she'll be happy about that.

'Okay, bye, honey,' Mom says.

I hang up and stare at the phone in my hands. It'd be too simple just to call her. What would I say, though? I've kept in touch with her friend Madison so that I can keep tabs on how Avery's doing. Just because she isn't mine doesn't mean I don't worry about her. I know my Mom's advice is going to ring in my head until I talk to Avery one last time.

Chapter 26

Avery

Feeling sorry for myself isn't working – neither is pretending my past will go away. It won't. Even if I transfer to a school in Alaska, and no one knows, I will know. And that's what I hate most. I hate living with the regret – having something I can never take back. It might sound strange, but I'm disappointed in myself, and I'm tired of living with that feeling.

Maybe that's what this little road trip will provide – the chance to think, to get away from everything for a few days, leave all my crappy baggage behind. When I return, I won't be the same girl. I'll know my mom, for one. And I'll work on forgiving myself. With each mile I drive, I'll leave my past behind me. So I took some sexy pictures with my boyfriend? I wasn't going to let that own me. Not anymore.

While other college kids are getting ready for a fun Friday night out, I'm preparing for a twelve hour drive to Denver. I'll stop for the night somewhere across the massively long state of Nebraska. That will put me into Denver tomorrow afternoon, and my mom, Jessica, or whatever I will call her, has asked me to come over and have lunch. The idea of meeting her is overwhelming, let alone seeing her home and sitting across from her over lunch. I may puke before I even drive the first mile of the trip.

Noah and Madison – just like my parents – are eager to join me on my road trip adventure, but I tell them the same thing. This is something I need to do alone. Maybe just to know that I am strong enough to face it.

It is late afternoon, but the sun is already preparing for its nightly hibernation. The streaks of golden sun lighting up the sky remind me I'll be driving in the dark soon and I need to get moving. I hitch my backpack higher on my shoulder and continue across campus to where my car waits. My car is right where I left it, but it's the guy standing next to the driver's door that gives me pause.

'Ja-Jase?' My tongue trips over his name, both from surprise at seeing him and from the ban I've imposed on speaking his name.

'Hi,' he returns carefully.

He's dressed casually in dark-washed jeans, a gray T-shirt and my favorite light blue hoodie that I liked to steal on occasion. Seeing him is physically painful. He's so handsome, and I'm reminded how comfortably we fit together. My body remains rooted to the sidewalk, because I know if I go to him, my head will rest perfectly in the crook of his neck, his T-shirt will smell like a mix of fabric softener and cologne, and if his arms circle around me I will feel safe.

I pull a shaky breath into my lungs. *What is he doing here?*

Jase takes a step closer. 'So you're really doing this?' My eyes must betray my confusion, because he adds, 'I talked to Madison.'

I nod. *Damn Madison.* I know they've been conversing about me in their shared lit class. I try not to read too much into it. 'Yep. She lives in Denver. We're meeting up tomorrow afternoon for lunch.' It explains how he knew where I was headed, but not what he's doing here with a duffle bag slung over his shoulder. 'Did you…need something?' I don't mean for it to sound so cold, clinical, yet it does.

'I'd like to come with you – like we talked about.'

I frown. 'That was before.'

'I know,' he adds quickly. 'But I'm the one who pushed you toward this, and it seems right that I should be with you when you go. Just because…of what happened…doesn't mean I'm going back on my word. I am your life coach, and I intend to see this project through.' He attempts a smile, but I'm not amused. I'm done feeling like his project.

I continue past him toward the car, unlocking my door to toss my backpack on the backseat. 'It's fine, Jase. I'm good with going alone.' I don't know what's with his weird sense of responsibility toward me. But I want a friend…or maybe a boyfriend…not a guardian.

'Avery,' his voice goes soft, and his eyes are glued on me. 'I'd like to come. I'm all packed.' He holds up the backpack he's carrying. 'Let me be there for you.'

Do I even want him on this trip? I have visions of myself cruising down the highway, singing along to the radio, and giving myself a nervous pep talk in the driveway before meeting my mom. Do I want an audience for what is sure to be an emotional trip? I have always imagined doing it alone.

Jase looks at me with hopeful eyes. I can't help but notice he's said nothing about *us* – about what him being here means. Why is he really here?

I take a deep breath and realize I do want him by my side, having his comfortable silence next to me, his warm hand to hold if I need it. It changes everything. I don't know what will happen between us, but there's no one else I'd rather have with me.

'Fine. Get in.'

He smiles. 'Want me to take the first driving shift?'

'No. I'll drive.' I'll need something to concentrate on other than him. We climb into the car and as soon as the doors are shut, his familiar scent washes over me. So much for concentrating.

*

Jase

I know she's surprised to see me, but I didn't expect her to actually consider sending me away. But I see the indecision in her eyes, the split-second of uncertainty before she says yes.

I settle in the passenger seat next to Avery and flip through the radio stations, asking what she's in the mood to listen to. She shrugs, noncommittal about anything, but I guess it's to be expected. I can't even imagine all the emotions she must feel embarking on this trip.

Avery drives slow and steady in the right lane of the highway. I don't complain though – I'm fine with letting her take things at her own pace. I'll probably have to drive tomorrow, knowing she'll likely be a jittery mess as the time approaches to meet her mom.

I realize I've never been in the car while she's driving, and though I usually prefer being the driver, watching her concentrate on the road is pretty cute. She gets a crease in her forehead and her little hands are gripping the wheel at ten and two. She also looks thinner, which I don't like. But she also looks more determined, more sure, and I do like that.

I sneak glances at Avery as we drive, and the images from those sexy photos flash through my mind. I hate remembering her that way. The raw feeling of shock and disgust when I first saw those pictures slices through me. I wanted to hit something, or someone. Fuck, I still do. I don't like associating the sweet, innocent girl I fell for with something so dirty. But that past is part of her, and I have to decide if it's something I can get over or not. Will I ever be able to look at her without remembering?

The hours tick by and as I watch the passing headlights, I wonder what the future holds for me and Avery.

*

Avery

We don't discuss my pornographic past, we don't talk about *us*. We just drive. Each hour carries us closer to Denver, and I can't help but feel further apart emotionally. The casual banter that used to flow so easily between us has been snatched away. This is what I'd always feared – getting close to someone, and then having it ripped away from me once my secret came out. That's why it's easier not to get too close. But nothing ventured, nothing gained and all that. Crap. I hate how in my head I get about Jase. I need to just let it go. Him being here doesn't mean anything…does it?

Jase yawns and stretches next to me, pulling my attention from the road over to him. 'When do you wanna stop?' he says around another yawn.

The clock on the dash informs me it's already after eleven. I've been driving for almost six hours. *Wow*. My neck is stiff and sore and cracks when I roll my shoulders. 'I just thought I'd pull into a motel off the highway, and crash. Sound okay to you?'

He nods. 'Sounds good.'

A few minutes later, Jase points out a sign for a motel. It's a cheap and probably run-down chain, but it'll do. I don't need anything fancy. I pull off onto the exit, more than ready to get out and stretch my legs.

As I navigate us toward the motel, Jase gestures to the string of fast food restaurants further down the road. 'Let's grab something to eat first. You're too thin, and I doubt you had dinner.'

I grin sheepishly. He's right. I haven't been eating well. Somehow food just doesn't taste like it used to. Most days I have to force myself to get something down, and today, with all the excitement, it completely slipped my mind. 'Sure. Burgers or subs?' I survey the restaurants around us.

Jase looks over at me, his eyes smiling on mine. 'I'm feeding you the biggest cheeseburger we can find. It wouldn't hurt to put a few pounds on you.'

I chuckle and shake my head at him. I'm nowhere near model-thin, but it's nice to hear his concern, just the same.

After polishing off cheeseburgers and fries, Jase and I check into the little motel he'd seen off the highway. An adjoining door separates our rooms, and though I want a shower and to crawl in bed, suddenly that door is all I can think about. Or more specifically, what's on the other side of it. I shouldn't allow myself to feel any hope, but I can't help wonder what Jase is thinking. I'm also worried about trusting myself with him.

Chapter 27

Jase

I've paced the room for the last fifteen minutes, trying to talk myself out of it. I heard her shower turn on – and then off, eight minutes later – and now she's probably getting ready for bed, but still I can't shake the desire to see her.

I take one last deep breath, willing myself just to let it go and move on, but I know I won't. It's why I'm on this trip. I can't give her up.

I tap my knuckles against the door and wait.

It's completely silent. Maybe she's already asleep. But a few seconds later, the door opens and Avery's standing before me in a white tank top and baggy pink pajama pants, bare feet and damp hair. Her simple beauty crashes against me like a wave. I want to push the hair from her shoulders and kiss a path up her neck, remembering how good she tastes.

'Hey,' I say brilliantly.

'Hi,' she returns, her voice soft and cautious.

I swallow down a wave of nerves, wondering what the fuck I say now. I should have thought this shit out. 'Can I come in?'

'Sure.' She takes a step back from the door.

Her room smells like her shampoo and the air is still dewy from the shower, which is not helping my train of thought.

140

Avery stands silently watching me. I do the only thing I can think to do: I step closer and place my hands against her waist, pulling her close. Avery looks up at me with curiosity in her eyes as my thumb lightly strokes the bare skin at her hip. I don't know what's happening, or what's left between us, all I know is that I need this. I need to erase all those vivid mental images of her with her ex. I need to make her mine. I'm in no mood to talk about my feelings. I just want her naked. I need to feel her skin. If that makes me an asshole, so be it.

I lower my mouth to hers, then stop. I won't force her into anything. I want to give her the chance to decide.

'Jase?' Her breath whispers across my mouth.

'Yeah?'

Her tongue dampens her bottom lip, but she doesn't say anything else, she just closes her eyes and waits for me to kiss her. I don't hesitate. I capture her mouth in a fierce kiss; a kiss I desperately hope chases away all the bad memories. Avery grips my shoulders, clinging to me, clawing at my biceps. Something primal and possessive bubbles up inside me. I push her back to the bed, helping her scramble onto the mattress. We're both breathless as we crash together again, kissing, struggling to get closer.

There are no words tonight. No over-analyzing shit. We are two bodies, attracted to each other and fulfilling a need so deep it can only be overcome one way. I want to be inside her. I'm desperate to claim her, but I don't have a condom and I doubt she does, either. I rip her pants down her legs and find her bare underneath. Her fingers work at the button on my jeans, trembling and unsure. I rise from the bed and remove my jeans and boxers. I stand proudly in front of her and watch as her gaze lowers to my insanely hard cock. I realize I've never been naked in front of her before. The desire in her eyes tells me she likes what she sees. I pull my shirt off next and join her on the bed once again.

Avery's eyes linger over me, taking in everything. Unable to slow the pace, I pull her up so I can remove her shirt. Her bra is the last article between us and I find the clasp at the middle of her back and free her of it. I toss it over the side of the bed with the rest of my clothes.

Avery climbs on top of me, straddling my hips and her bare flesh presses into me, the tiny rotations of her hips driving me crazy. My head drops back on the pillow and a groan escapes the back of my throat.

Being naked with Avery is a bad idea. Capital fucking B. Her bare skin is so soft and smells so good, I have to taste her. I sit up so I can reach her mouth, and kiss her deeply. Avery matches my pace, her tongue massaging mine. The only sounds are skin sliding against skin, heavy breathing and the occasional soft moan from Avery. It's making me crazy.

My fingers grip her waist, holding her still against me. I can feel how wet she is and it's not helping my erection. I'm going to embarrass myself if she doesn't stop grinding against me soon.

Kissing a damp path down her throat, I stop to nibble her collar-bone before tilting my head to capture her breast in my mouth. Avery arches forward, groaning loudly in the too quiet room. My hands leave her waist, as I decide to momentarily trust her not to send me over the edge. One hand glides up her spine, curling around the back of her neck to lower her mouth to mine, while my other hand reaches between us to massage the sensitive nub of flesh she's trying desperately to rub against my groin.

Avery's head drops back and she growls with pleasure as I glide my fingers over her tender skin, sending her closer and closer to release. I attack her exposed throat with kisses, biting into the skin and sucking hard enough to leave a mark as my fingers increase their rhythm. Avery responds, but not at all like I expect her to. She scrambles from my lap, breathless, her eyes wide with fear.

'Babe?' I pull a deep breath into my lungs. *Did I do something wrong?* She doesn't answer, but her eyes fill with tears. *What the fuck?* 'Did I hurt you?'

She shakes her head.

'Tell me what I did.' I reach for her hand, but she pulls away from me, climbing off the bed to stand on shaky legs.

My overheated body struggles to catch up to my brain. We're still both naked, though my erection is quickly catching up to the problem. I grab the sheet from the bed and wrap it around her shoulders, and then step into my boxers. 'Tell me what happened.' My voice is firm, but I don't care. She was having a good time, about to come, I think, and then she just snapped.

Avery swallows visibly and tugs the blanket tighter around herself. 'I'm sorry. That was just too much for me. This – whatever that was – I can't. I just need to focus on me. I need to get through tomorrow. I can't handle this with you *and* the idea of meeting my mother tomorrow. I need to pick my battles.'

Shit fuck. I shouldn't have come in here with one thing on my mind – to make us both forget. Avery has bigger things on her shoulders right now. Maybe she wanted to talk, have someone beside her to listen to her feelings, hell, maybe she wanted to be left alone. Either way, I've fucked up. Again.

'I'm sorry.' I pull up my jeans. 'I wasn't thinking.'

She clutches the blanket around her shoulders and watches me get dressed.

The moment between us has passed, and I can sense she wants me gone. I pull my T-shirt over my head. 'I'll go. I'm sorry, I shouldn't have come. Just get some sleep.'

She nods and I disappear through the door to my own room.

*

Avery

I am shaking when Jase leaves. I sink to the floor, leaning against the door he just exited. I can't believe he just left...I know I freaked out, but I just needed a second. Having him take control like that was too reminiscent of Brent and I hate feeling out of control. My heart is slamming against my chest as I process the fact that he only wants the physical with me. Is it because of my background – that's how he sees me? It's the reputation I've earned, but I thought Jase, of all people, would understand I'm not that girl anymore. My abandonment issues had clouded my judgment, and that's all much too close to home right now.

I have no idea where Jase and I stand. Is this just physical for him? Does he want something more? Is he over my past? The questions won't stop, and I suddenly can't breathe. I hope that Jase, who knows about my past, would understand that some things will be uncomfortable for me. But his mouth was demanding, his hands insistent, and he'd nearly pushed me over the edge before I got control back. I don't trust him not to hurt me again. To leave me high and dry when he stops and thinks about the pictures again.

Once I get my breathing under control, I get dressed and curl up in the big bed, hugging a pillow against my chest to combat the empty feeling inside. It does little good, because the pillow smells like him. It's comforting, but it also makes the throb in my chest more painful.

I spend the night tossing and turning against the lumpy mattress, begging my brain to shut off so I can sleep. Sleep finally comes, but it's restless.

In the morning, neither Jase nor I speak about last night. We grab breakfast from the lobby – bitter tasting coffee and stale muffins – and hit the road. I can tell he regrets coming with me. Hell, he probably thinks I'm an all-out basket case. And maybe I am. But I can't focus on everything that's gone wrong between us right now. Today is the today I've been waiting for all my life. I push away the dark, swirling thoughts about Jase's hasty departure last night and climb into the car.

After two hours of driving, I pull off the highway with the excuse of needing to fill up the gas tank, but really I just need a break. My knuckles are sore from gripping the steering wheel and my emotions are all over the place. Luckily, Jase doesn't comment that I still have half a tank, he just gets out of the car and begins pumping the gas, then offers to drive the last leg of the trip. I merely nod and shove the keys at him.

Jase's expression is guarded and I can't tell what he's thinking. But I try not to worry about that, and instead slump into the passenger seat while he runs inside to the convenience store. He returns a few minutes later with bottles of water and soda and a few chocolate bars.

He gets in beside me and dumps everything onto my lap. 'You should have some sugar…it'll make you feel better.'

I nod and tear into a Hershey's bar, taking a small nibble from the corner. Jase is right, the sugar floods my system and perks me up the slightest bit. I finish the whole chocolate bar and drink half the soda as he takes over driving. We're getting close now – the GPS on my phone says only a couple more turns before we reach our final destination. It sounds ominous.

Jase is silent, but I can see him stealing glances at me from the corner of his eye as he drives. We still haven't talked about last night. I wonder if I should feel embarrassed for practically kicking him out of my room naked and very obviously turned on, but that's not even making the cut right now. My entire being is absorbed by the fact I'm about to meet my mom.

Eventually we pull onto a tree-lined street. The homes are small, but well-maintained. It's surreal to finally see where she lives – to think, if things had been different, this is where I could've grown up. I watch the addresses as we pass and my heartbeat builds to a staggering level in my chest.

Jase slows to a stop and parks in front of a single-story brick home with a paved brick walkway cutting through the front yard. 'We're here.'

Chapter 28

Jase

Watching Avery meet her mom for the first time is physically painful. I can feel the jittery excitement, the thick awkward air hanging around us as they take each other in, the moment Avery decides they should hug and reaches out in a sloppy attempt at a one-armed embrace. God, I wish I could make this moment easier on her. Jessica, her mom, hugs her back, flinging both arms around. They sob onto each other's shoulders. A tight feeling invades my chest as I watch them.

There's no denying the resemblance. Avery and her mom share many of the same features: their long, wavy auburn-colored hair, the bright emerald eyes and smattering of freckles across the bridge of their noses. Watching them hug is more emotionally taxing than I would have thought. I'd approached this whole thing with Avery in mind – being there for her was my goal. I didn't expect to be overcome at the sight of their reunion. Yet, I can't deny that watching a mother and child lay eyes on each other for the first time in nineteen years doesn't pull at something deep inside me. My chest gets tight, and I can't help but think of my own parents right now. Even if we've gone through some messed up stuff together, I'm still glad they're my parents. I can't imagine the emotions of knowing you were put up for adoption. It makes me want to hold Avery, to kiss away her tears. I vow never to fuck up again with her like I did last night. She deserves more, and if she'll let me try again, I intend to give her everything.

After several minutes of hugging, sobbing and pointing out similarities, Jessica releases her hold on Avery and I introduce myself as Avery's friend. Feeling generous, she gives me a solid hug too. Apparently the atmosphere is contagious. Jessica leads us up the walkway toward the house and I find Avery's hand, squeezing it in mine. She wipes at her eyes and gives me a shaky smile. I'm so glad she didn't insist on doing this alone.

Jessica's house is small, but nicely decorated. The living room holds two couches separated by a coffee table tackled with books. She directs me and Avery to take a seat. I let Avery choose her spot, then sit down next to her. Jessica sits across from us, and silence fills the room as the enormity of this moment sinks in.

'Sooo…' I chuckle nervously, attempting to help jumpstart the conversation that neither of them seems to know how to begin. 'Jessica, what do you do?'

She swallows and tears her eyes away from Avery briefly. 'Oh, right.' She smiles warmly. 'I teach high school English.'

Avery's eyes widen. 'English was my favorite subject in high school.'

Jessica continues and we learn she isn't married and doesn't have any other children. She lives alone, aside from a cat, and loves to read – another thing she and Avery have in common. I think Avery's relieved to find she's so normal. I know I am. I would have felt terrible for Avery to discover her mom was a weirdo.

Jessica prepares sandwiches for lunch and they catch up while we eat. I notice they have the same mannerisms – fidgeting with their napkins, tucking hair behind their ears, even their posture is the same. It's uncanny.

After lunch, Avery shares some photos from her childhood, and it's the first time I've seen her dads. They seem like a happy family.

Jessica asks some questions, but doesn't pry. She keeps the conversation more in the here and now – what Avery's majoring in, how she likes her classes, things like that. Avery, taking her cues from Jessica, doesn't delve into the past either, though she's got to be curious about Jessica's decision to give her up for adoption, about her birthfather. I know I am. But perhaps there's a certain etiquette to these things, and the heavier topics will come at the next meeting.

All too soon, it's late afternoon, and Avery and I prepare to leave. Jessica hugs us each one last time with teary eyes and tells Avery to email or call anytime. As soon as we're outside the door, I pull Avery into my arms. Her breath releases in a sigh and she relaxes against me. 'I'm proud of you,' I whisper. Her arms tighten around my waist.

Avery's silent and contemplative on the drive to the hotel. We plan to spend one night in Denver and then make the long drive back on Sunday.

When we reach the hotel, Avery looks exhausted. 'Thanks for being here.'

I can't help but reach out to touch her. I push the hair back from her face, stroking her cheek softly. 'Anytime, Whistle. You doing okay?'

She smiles at the nickname and nods. 'Yeah. It went much better than I expected.'

I have to agree, and I'm sure she was mentally preparing herself for the worst too. Avery yawns loudly and I chuckle. She has a content smile on her face, but I can tell today emotionally drained her, and if she was as restless as I was last night, she's got to be exhausted. 'Why don't you go take a nap, and then we'll go out to dinner later?'

She nods. 'Okay.'

We part ways, Avery goes into her room and I head into mine. I lie down on the bed trying to clear my head. Only I can't concentrate. All I can think about is the girl on the other side of the door, and wonder if maybe she needs me. I shuffle to the door separating our rooms and knock softly. It opens right away, like Avery was waiting right there.

'Hi,' she says, softly.

'Hey. You want some company?'

She nods and motions me inside. Avery collapses onto the bed and scoots over, making room for me. We lie side by side and stare up at the bumpy stucco ceiling.

'Today was pretty heavy, huh?' I ask.

'Yeah.'

'How do you feel?'

She takes her time responding. 'It went better than I ever hoped for. She's nice and normal.'

I nod, encouraging her. I want to reach out and take her hand again, but I hesitate. I don't want her thinking I'm in here for any other reason than just to be here for her and to talk. 'Is she what you imagined? You look just like her.'

Avery sighs and continues, 'Yeah, that was kinda cool. I always wondered if I looked like her. But that sadness inside me didn't just vanish when I met her. I guess you can't erase nineteen years' worth of being absent – of giving me up in the first place.'

This time I don't hesitate. I take her hand and lace her fingers between mine. She turns her head to the side and gives me a shaky smile. 'Are you okay?'

She nods. 'Yeah. I didn't want to ask her about any of that this first time. I didn't want to spoil the moment, you know?'

I give her hand a squeeze and wait for her to continue.

'And I guess it just cemented that my dads really are my family.'

'They love you,' I say, remembering the photos I saw of Avery as a little girl in between the two beaming-with-pride men. She was clearly adored and very much wanted by them.

'I know. They wanted to come today. And so did Madison and Noah, for that matter.'

'But you let me,' I say.

Avery doesn't respond, she just watches me while the weight of the moment between us blooms into more. The air around us is heavy, and I wish things could go back to being easy and carefree. But I know she needs me now more than ever.

A single tear slips from the corner of her eye. I'm not surprised; I'd been wondering how she was still holding it together. Dampness swims in her eyes, but she doesn't look away. I rub the back of her hand lightly with my thumb. 'It's okay. Let it out. I've got you.'

She does, turning to fit herself in my arms, and sobs into my neck, her chest heaving with each ragged breath. Each cry that breaks through her throat cuts me open. I hold her through it all, knowing there's no place I'd rather be.

Chapter 29

Avery

I sob for all the lost time, the memories that we'd never create, the mother that abandoned me as a baby. I cry for a life that could have been. For the choice my mom had to make and at such a young age, and for the circumstances that led to that decision.

Life is a crapshoot. We've all been dealt a hand that we have no choice but to play – my mom by getting pregnant too young, me with simply the circumstances I was born into.

After meeting her face to face, seeing how normal she is, I'm not immature enough to believe she'd given me up because I was a bad baby. No. She'd made the best decision she could for me and for herself. But that didn't make this any easier. She'd done the most selfless thing she could do. She'd given me to two loving parents who desperately wanted a child. It broke my heart. There's grief and loss mixed in with happiness and joy. It's all too much.

Jase just holds me. He lets me completely fall apart. He doesn't say anything, other than making calming sounds meant to soothe. He rubs my back in slow circles and rocks me silently against his chest. I can't even let myself hope what his presence might mean. He's here now, all solid and warm, and holding me. It's not nearly enough, but it'll do. For now.

By the time I'm all cried out, my throat is raw and Jase's T-shirt is soaked with my tears, but he doesn't seem the least bit concerned about this shirt. His hand continues its soothing path, rubbing slow circles between my shoulder blades while my breathing returns to normal.

Jase

When her tears finally stop, little unsteady hiccups continue to rasp in her chest for several minutes more. Avery eventually lifts her head from my shoulder and blinks up at me, wiping away the remnants of her makeup.

'I'm sorry,' she croaks, her voice raw from crying.

'No. Don't be. I'm glad you let it out, and I'm glad I could be here for you.'

She nods. 'Thanks, Jase.'

'Anytime, Whistle.'

Confusion crosses her face at hearing the nickname I haven't used in a while. She's wondering the same thing I am – about us. About where we stand now.

She sits up on the bed, completely disentangling herself from me. The loss of warmth from her body next to mine is unwelcome, but I resist the urge to tug her back to me.

'I'm gonna take a shower,' she says.

Her face is red, her chest splotchy and her hair is a tangled, matted mess--the strands framing her face slightly damp from her tears. 'Yeah, okay.' The warm water will soothe her some, I hope. 'I'll go out and pick us up dinner. We can eat here in bed if you're okay with that, and watch TV.'

She climbs from the bed. 'Yeah, low key sounds great.'

I didn't figure she'd be up for going out someplace. I take the keys from the bedside table and watch as Avery disappears into the bathroom, closing the door behind her. When I hear the water turn on, I have to fight the urge to go in after her.

I return a little while later with bags of Chinese takeout. Dressed in a white tank and pink cotton pants, Avery sits cross-legged in the center of the bed. 'Hi,' she says.

Her smile is back, so I can only assume the shower helped. Her hair is still damp, but combed neatly and secured in a braid across her shoulder. It makes her look younger. Beautiful. Food is suddenly the last thing on my mind.

'What'd you get us? It smells good.'

I set the bag on the bedside table and begin unloading the paper cartons. 'Chinese. Hope that's okay.'

'Yeah, that's perfect.'

We eat spicy noodles, spring rolls and almond chicken while watching a mindless comedy on cable. By the time we're full, Avery is openly laughing at the movie. I throw the leftovers away in my adjoining room and close the door. I'm hopeful we'll share a bed tonight. Even if nothing else happens, I just want to be near her. And I figure we won't want to breathe in the smell of old Chinese food all night.

Avery has stacked all the pillows from my bed and hers up against the headboard and is lounging against them when I return from brushing my teeth. 'You're looking quite comfortable there.'

She crosses her legs at the ankle and smiles, like a princess perched on her throne. Now that we're done eating, the room is too quiet, too full of her. Suddenly I don't know what to do with myself. Avery just continues watching me with wide green eyes.

I hesitate at the end of the bed, and rub the back of my neck, waiting for her to give me some indication she wants me to stay. Although she's commandeered all my pillows so…. 'You're holding my pillows hostage… does that mean you want me here?'

'Maybe I just really like pillows…' She wiggles against the mountain behind her, making herself comfortable. 'Kidding. Of course you're staying.' She pats the bed beside her 'You being here means a lot.'

I wish I knew what she's thinking. I cross the room to sit beside her on the bed. 'You doing better?' I ask, though I can see she is.

The glow in her cheeks is back, her eyes are bright and happy. Whatever she has worked through in the last couple of hours, I can only hope has been helped by my presence. The feeling is addicting. I just like being near her, and I'm not going anywhere as long as she wants me here.

Avery scoots over, making room for me on the bed, and moves closer to sink against the pillows. We're half-sitting, half-lying side by side.

'Should we talk about my past … indiscretions?' she asks, staring at the ceiling.

I hate how she's had to live with so much on her shoulders. But she's right. We do need to talk about that. I wonder if she's going to start, because I have no clue what to say. She grips her hands in front of her looking nervous.

I take a deep breath and start. 'Listen, Avery, I can get over the pictures. We've all made stupid mistakes. But I don't like feeling lied to.' She doesn't say anything, just keeps looking straight up at the ceiling, her expression neutral. 'The main thing holding me back is that you're not who I thought you were. I can't escape the feeling like I've been fooled by you. Do I even know the real Avery? Was it all a carefully constructed cover up, or did I see the real you?'

Her shoulders straighten, and she seems to draw some inner strength. 'You saw the real me. The messy, scared shitless me trying to figure out a way to move past it.'

'When I first met you, you were running and I just wanted to help. Seeing you crouched behind that dumpster…shit, Avery.' I take a deep breath, letting it creep out of my lungs slowly.

'It's fine, Jase. You don't need to explain. You needed a little project to distract you from the issues with your mom – fine. Mission accomplished. But guess what? I don't want to be someone's project. I'm done being broken. And I'm done hiding from my past. I've made mistakes. I'm not perfect. I need someone who can deal with that.'

'You were never a project, and we both know it. I wasn't involved with you for some noble purpose. I loved watching your eyes light up, seeing you let go, making you blush when I made dirty comments. I made it my mission to see you smile.'

'Well, I'm officially done hiding. It didn't do me any good anyway. And when I dated Brent, I wasn't the same girl that I am now. He was my first crush; I wanted to impress him, to fit in and be a little reckless…obviously you can see how well that worked out for me. It was a stupid mistake that I can't take back, Jase.'

'Fuck your past. It won't own us. I can't think straight without you. I miss you. I want you back, babe.'

I'm sorry about all she had to endure. I'm sorry about her fucktard ex. I'm sorry she'd taken those pictures. But I can push it all aside. I want this girl. I want her for my own. End of story. The world can fuck off for all I care. She's mine.

'Whistle, I'm going to kiss you now.'

The tightness across my shoulders lessens for the first time in weeks. I lean in and kiss her, soft and tenderly, my lips skimming across hers. I nip at her bottom lip, drawing it into my mouth, and she lets out a soft exhale at the sudden contact. I'm torn…I want her, have wanted her for so long, and now she's mine and we're alone together in a hotel, but I don't want to rush her.

Avery, having not gotten the memo about my decision to take things slow, pushes her hands under my shirt and rubs them along my chest and stomach. Even the simplest of touches from her are amazing. Finding her courage, she climbs onto my lap and strad-dles me. I grip her waist and continue kissing her, not wanting to rush things, but also not willing to give up this moment. Her hands stop at the waistband of my jeans, and with trembling fingers, she begins working at the button. It takes every ounce of self-control I possess to find her hands and stop her.

'Avery.' I breathe against her mouth and she pulls back just a fraction, her eyes searching mine. I hate that just when she finds herself and initiates physical contact between us, I have to stop her.

I press my palms to her cheeks, give her a firm kiss on the forehead and remove her from my lap. Her eyes betray her confusion and hurt.

'As badly as I want this, I want to do things right with you. I've never even taken you out on a proper date.'

'Are you turning me down?' She pouts.

I question myself for the briefest of moments. Especially since my pants have grown considerably tighter. 'I will possess you baby, and when I do, it'll be worth the wait.'

She chuckles softly, a faint blush coloring her chest. 'This is quite the role reversal. I'm ready for sex, and now you're not.'

I groan and adjust my erection. 'Behave.' I move the pillows into place and pull her down against me so we're lying side by side, looking at each other. I don't even want to turn off the light to sleep, so I can just watch her, but I know I should. Once we're plunged into darkness, her hand slides into mine, and she lets out a soft sigh.

The journey we're on together is rocky, but I think it's led us to the right place. Avery is stronger, more sure, and I'm not the guy I was. The partying scene, meaningless hookups – I'd wanted more all along and now I've found it. Avery is my *more*. I want to be better for her, be her everything. A twinge of regret pinches inside me as I realize I'll have to find a way to tell Avery that I was with Stacia when she and I weren't seeing each other. But I'll worry about that later' for now I just hold her.

Chapter 30

Avery

'Break a leg!' I squeeze Madison and Noah one last time before they slip out of our dorm room. They have to be to the theater early for all the opening night preparations, which leaves me plenty of time to get ready for my date tonight. Jase has made reservations at an upscale restaurant, but first we're going to watch the play Madison and Noah are in. I grab my shower stuff and shuffle off to the communal bathrooms.

An hour later, I'm squeaky clean, shaved, made up and dressed. I sit down at my laptop to type a quick response to the email I got earlier from Jessica. It's been a month since we met face to face, and we've emailed back and forth several times. Our relationship has evolved into long emails full of random thoughts, deep-seated feelings and life happenings. It's nice. Even my dads are really cool about encouraging my relationship with her. I check the time, stuff my phone into the back pocket of my jeans, add some lip gloss and slip into my bright pink ballet flats.

I'm waiting on the sidewalk outside my dorm just as Jase pulls up in his sleek black car. He stops and his face breaks into a smile when he climbs from the car to greet me.

'Beautiful…' He leans down and whispers, his lips brushing past the skin near my ear. It sends a tingle down the back of my neck, settling at the base of my spine. As hard as this past month has been resisting giving into the physical with Jase, I think it is exactly what we need. It gives us the chance to actually just date and get to know each other better without sex complicating things. Things between us are great, though. Complete open and honesty, which feels really good. But the slow build between us physically has reached epic proportions. He will be mine tonight. Period.

Our dinner reservations are at an upscale sushi restaurant that has recently opened and has been getting good reviews. Jase assures me that jeans will be fine, but I'd paired them with a dressy cream-colored top trimmed in lace.

Jase's eyes slip from mine, dropping lower to survey me from head to toe. I squirm under his gaze and clamp my thighs together, praying that I'll make it through the play and dinner without trying to rip his clothes off. Or my own. Hmm, that could work. We have thirty minutes before the play starts…

'Avery?' he asks, pulling my mind from the gutter it has gleefully dived into.

Keeping my thoughts from wandering to later and the little scrap of black lace panties he'll discover is becoming increasingly difficult. 'Yes?'

He smirks, shaking his head as though he's reading my mind the entire time. Jase is sex on a stick in a pair of fitted dark jeans and a navy blue button up shirt that brings out the deep blue of his eyes. His hair is an absolute disaster, just the way I like it – a perfect mess. My fingers could roam to their heart's content and it wouldn't make the least bit of difference.

Crossing the distance between us, Jase pulls me tight against him and drops a sweet kiss to my mouth. 'Ready?' He smiles down at me, sparkling eyes playful and hungry. I'm ready to skip dinner and get onto desert, but I merely nod. We have a play to go to first, and I can't stand Madison and Noah up. They've adopted Jase into our circle over the past month and so of course we'll be there at their opening show.

We arrive at the theater in plenty of time to grab seats near the front. Watching Madison and Noah in the school's flirty reproduction of Grease is so fun, the two hours pass quickly. Noah as Rizzo is over-the-top-goodness, and I can't wait to hug him for not only winning the role, but for owning it. At the end, Jase stands and cheers for them along with me, and we fight our way backstage through the throngs of people to give them both a hug.

Jase has taken his mission of bringing me out on proper dates seriously, and after the play, we're hand in hand, heading across town to make the dinner reservations.

The restaurant is sleek and stylish and the sushi is divine, but sitting across from Jase at an intimate table for two, and feeling his eyes move across me is too much. Using my uncooperative chopsticks, I've tried as delicately as possible to wrestle pieces of sushi into my mouth in the most ladylike way possible.

Jase pops another piece of the spicy tuna roll into his mouth, chewing thoughtfully as he watches me. He's in no hurry, and I wonder if he's feeling any of the same fire I am. But I know he is. Intensity lights his eyes as he watches me. He finishes chewing and places his chopsticks beside his plate. 'Dessert?'

I'm ready to kick him under the table, but I fix on my most polite smile. 'No thanks. You?'

Jase chuckles, his eyes raking over my skin as he takes his time answering. 'Yes. Once we get home, I'd very much like some dessert.'

Gah… He is so overwhelming. Just knowing what's going to happen later between us makes my thighs tremble. I am more than ready for him now.

Jase settles our check, then guides me from the restaurant with his hand on the small of my back. It's an innocent touch, but he's hardly touched me all night, so the contact feels like an unspoken promise for more.

I was never like this with Brent. I'm ready, confident and sure. I'm sure about Jase.

When we get to Jase's, we're all hands and smiles and maybe even a few giggles on my part as we weave through the bodies. I'm thankful that he has zero interest in hanging out downstairs where the party rages on. He wants to be alone as badly as I do.

On our way to the stairs, Stacia places her hand on his chest and stops him. She staggers just a bit in her too high heels, before pulling her hand back.

'You two are back together?' Stacia laughs, too shrill and obvious.

I hold my chin high, refusing to let the fact that she saw my dirty little secret make me feel like damaged goods. If Jase is over it, then so am I.

'Drop it, Stac,' Jase warns, his voice tight and not amused.

Stacia grins devilishly, looking back and forth between Jase and I. 'You didn't tell her, did you?'

Shit. My stomach drops. 'Tell me what?'

Stacia laughs again. 'Never mind.' She smiles sweetly, wedging herself in between Jase and me as she passes so she can brush up against his chest.

Jase looks like he's about to hit something.

'Jase?'

He takes my hand and pulls me toward the stairs. All the heat and passion for our night together disappears and is replaced by a terrible nagging feeling. What isn't he telling me? What happened between him and Stacia?

Jase

I know I should've come clean before now. It's part of the reason why I didn't let our physical relationship go too far yet. Knowing that I still hadn't told her about my night with Stacia while we weren't talking held me back. I know Avery won't like it, and since we've agreed to complete honesty, I also know it makes me a jackass.

Once we reach my room, I shut the door behind us and turn to face her. Her hands are balled into fists, like she's bracing herself.

'Sit down, babe.'

She looks unsure, but slips off her shoes and crosses the room to sit on the edge of my bed. I pull a deep breath into my lungs, trying to find the words to explain this mess in a way that doesn't cause her to flip out. I sit down beside her and take her hand. It's limp. Shit. This isn't going to go well. 'When you and I…weren't talking…Stacia started coming around again.'

Her eyes betray her emotions, and begin to fill with tears even before I get to the heart of the story.

'We got pretty drunk one night…and um…' Shit. I can't say it.

'Tell me,' she whispers, her voice broken.

'We didn't have sex, but…' I pause, drawing another breath. 'She sort of started to go down on me….'

Her eyes fly to mine. I remember the time that I admitted to Avery that was my favorite, and I know she's remembering that too. I also know she's fully aware that it's something she and I haven't even done together. I feel like a complete prick. I never want to see this look in her eyes again.

She swallows roughly. 'I see.'

'Whistle, I'm sorry, but we weren't talking…'

She rips her hand from mine and stands suddenly. 'We weren't talking because you didn't want me, because you thought I was cheap and easy because of those stupid pictures. But you know what? You're no better than I am!' She grabs her purse and slips her feet back into her shoes. 'I need to go home.'

'Avery…wait…'

'Don't touch me!' A sob breaks from her throat and she pulls out of my grasp.

'At least let me drive you home. I'll be worried about you.'

She shakes her head. 'No. I'll call someone.' She fishes her phone out and dials. 'Madison,' she sobs. 'Come get me. I'm at Jase's…Yeah.'

Avery ends the call and leaves, jogging down the stairs.

Shit fuck.

I won't fuck this up again. I won't wait another few weeks without talking to her, like after our last fight. I need to make this right tonight. I race downstairs after her, but she's nowhere to be found in the sea of bodies. Heading out into the cool night air, I search the back deck, where I know she's hidden before. But it's occupied by a couple groping each other. Avery's gone.

I fish my keys from my pocket and cross around the side of my house, heading straight for my car. I can't leave things like this between us. Won't. We've wasted too much time already. My car is blocked in by three cars in our driveway, and I know trying to find the vehicle's owners will be pointless. I can't wait.

I race across campus to her dorm, arriving breathless from the three mile jog. I have to wait for someone to let me in, but get lucky and slip in behind a group of guys returning for the night. A few minutes later, I'm knocking on her door, praying she's going to answer.

Madison pulls the door open just a crack, her face a frown. 'Yes?'

'Is Avery here?'

'She doesn't want to see you.' She pushes the door closed, but my foot wedged in the doorframe keeps it from closing.

'I need to talk to her, please. Avery,' I call out.

Madison rolls her eyes, giving in, and lets me enter the room. 'Just talk to him. I can't handle you two,' she informs Avery.

My Whistle is curled up in her narrow bed, hugging a pillow to her chest. And she's been crying. Pain stabs at my chest. Fuck.

Madison grabs her purse. 'I'm going to Noah's.' The door clicks behind her.

Making no move to get any closer, I just watch her. Her eyes are guarded and her hands clutch the pillow tighter.

'Avery?' I swallow the lump in my throat, praying she'll listen to what I have to say. 'Can we talk?'

'What is there to say?' She shifts on the bed so she's sitting, but she keeps the pillow hugged to her chest, a physical barrier between us. 'It's your favorite, right? And I wasn't giving it to you, so...' She doesn't finish, but her eyes drop to the bed in front of her.

'Avery.' I make my move, getting as close as I dare. I kneel down at the edge of the bed, so we're eye-level. 'I am sooo sorry. That was a huge mistake. I was just feeling hurt and betrayed that you hadn't told me, and as bad as it sounds, I didn't care about anything else in that moment because I thought I had lost you. So when Stacia started undoing my belt...'

Avery's hand flies up to stop me. 'I don't need a play by play. God, what's wrong with you?'

Christ. 'I'm sorry, you're right. I just...I'm so sorry. If I could take that night back, I would. And I wanted to tell you. That night in Denver in the hotel, I wanted to tell you, but you were dealing with enough...'

She blinks up at me. 'Is this why we haven't...?'

'Gone farther physically?'

She nods.

'Yeah. I wanted to make sure everything was out in the open with us first.'

'I see.' She tucks her legs underneath her.

I want to reach for her hand. So bad. But I remain kneeling beside the bed. 'Tell me what you're thinking. Please.'

Her green gaze is piercing and cuts into my very soul. 'You're right. Finding out stuff from someone else sucks.'

I nod. And each time it's been Stacia, which I know is particularly annoying considering she's my ex. 'I'm sorry you had to hear it from her. Everything in the future comes straight from us. No more secrets.'

She shakes her head. 'You said that last time, even while you knew you should've told me this. How can I trust you?'

'Because. I love you, baby. You're mine, and I'm done playing games. I'm done hurting you. I'll give you anything and everything. I'll keep you safe and take care of your every need.'

'Crap.' A lopsided grin graces her mouth, curving it up on one side. 'Jase…' her voice has a pleading quality to it. Whatever she wants, she can have.

'What, baby? I love you.' I take her hands and bring them to my mouth, kissing the back of each one, then her wrists and palms. 'It's the God's honest truth.'

Her smile goes wider. 'I do like hearing that, but maybe if you could tell me a little more…'

'Like that I love the way you taste? The way your hair smells, and how sweet you are. I love how you burst into laughter at random times. I love how I make you blush, that my mom loves you, that you're smart and hardworking, genuine, and so loving…' Her cheeks glow with each compliment, and I pepper kisses along her wrists and fingertips.

Her smile is full and inviting at this point. I remove the pillow from her lap and join her on the bed, so I can pull her into my arms. I've known for a while, but I haven't told her. I'm not sure why, but it's clear from her teary-eyed look that she feels the same way, even if she doesn't say it back right now. I hold her against me, hugging her tight and loving the way her body feels against mine. Protectiveness swirls inside me and I vow not to hurt this girl again.

A knock on the door interrupts us and a second later, Madison peeks her head inside. 'Is it safe to come in?'

She has Noah in tow, and they don't wait for an answer. Avery and I separate as Madison flings her purse onto her bed and Noah flops down onto the futon. 'I knew you guys would make up.'

I lean into Avery, breathing in her scent and whisper, 'Sleepover at my place?'

She pulls back just slightly to meet my eyes and nods.

Thank you, God.

Chapter 31

Jase

Madison gives us a ride back to my place, and the reduced number of cars outside tells me the party has died down a bit. Once inside, I guide Avery straight for the staircase, not wanting anyone or anything to get in our way this time. I see from the corner of my eye that Stacia is still here, and her smug grin falls when she sees my grip on Avery's hand. Too bad. She's going to have to get over it, because Avery's not going anywhere. I need this girl in my life. We've made plans for our families to meet this winter, to be together during spring break, and I hope every weekend in between too. If her past isn't going to stop us, my ex-girlfriend certainly isn't going to, either.

Avery's hand tightens around mine and she dutifully follows me. I know she isn't going to let Stacia interfere again. I'm proud of my girl.

I pause at the stairs, realizing maybe it's rude to drag her directly to my bedroom. It is Saturday night, and there is a party going on. Maybe she wants to hang out for a bit. 'Do you want a drink or anything?'

She looks at me like I've just asked her if she likes murdering puppies. 'Get your hot ass up those stairs and quit stalling.'

Whoa. That was fucking hot. 'Yes ma'am.' She doesn't have to tell me twice. If she's even half as ready for this as me, she's probably ready to combust. I know I am.

Once we're inside my room, she's instantly in my arms, pressing her body to mine and kissing me. I kick the door shut behind us. I need to calm myself so this isn't over before it starts. I don't want to embarrass myself. And I need to remember this is her first time.

Moving Avery to my bed, I give her shoulders a playful shove, and she falls back on the mattress, giggling. Unable to stay away, I quickly join her. 'You're gorgeous when you laugh like that.'

Her face gets serious and I'm about to ask her what's wrong, but her fingers fumble at the button on my jeans and I've suddenly forgotten how to talk.

Avery

I want to do this. I need to do this, but I'm hit with a wave of nerves as I tug Jase's black boxer briefs down on his hips. He lifts slightly off the bed to help me. His thick erection bobs free, greeting me, and I suddenly tense. I haven't really seen it in the light like this before. It's bigger than I was expecting. Wrapping my hand around him, Jase sucks in a breath and reclines against the bed. His flesh is hard and warm, and I can't resist stroking my hand from the base to the tip, squeezing lightly. Jase groans softly, his eyes locked on mine. I climb off the bed, and situate myself on my knees in front of him. Might as well get the full experience. But before I can touch him again, he grasps my shoulders with both hands.

'What are you doing?' He's breathless. It's adorable.

'I thought it was obvious.' For some reason, I feel all proud and powerful, even though I'm the one on my knees.

'Avery, you do not have to do this.' He gaze is serious, like he's legitimately concerned. But I'm not doing this for him. This is for me.

'Jase, I want to.' I do. I want to see what all the fuss is about. If I don't like it, I'll stop. Without waiting for him to respond, I grasp him firmly in one hand. Lowering my head until my mouth meets warm flesh, I give him a slow French kiss, swirling my tongue around the swollen head. Jase's low moan is the sexiest sound I've ever heard. Emboldened by his obvious satisfaction, I draw him into my mouth, leaving nothing on the table. I kiss, lick, suck and stroke until Jase is rocking his hips and cursing under his breath. It's a very powerful feeling knowing I'm the one making him feel these things.

Jase's hand on my jaw pulls my eyes up to his. 'Babe,' his voice is a raspy whisper. 'You need to stop.'

Pride swells within me, knowing that I've brought him so close to the edge. He helps me up from the floor and I lie down next to him. I'm so glad that I waited for Jase for my first time. I'm not even nervous as Jase removes my jeans and panties. I pull my top over my head, and he unclasps my bra. After we're each undressed, we slide under the sheets and continue kissing. I wrap my leg over his hip and curl my body into his. I can feel his hardness pressing against my lower belly.

'Jase,' I whimper.

Without making an awkward production of things, Jase reaches for a condom and puts it on, kissing me while he does. Knowing there's nothing standing in our way now and that I'm about to have him pushes me onward. I grip his shoulder with one hand, the other tucked uselessly between us, but I clutch at his hip. Slowly, carefully, Jase positions himself against me. We're lying side by side, eyes open, watching each other and kissing as he slides inside me. I can feel him press forward and begin to penetrate me, and though it's slightly uncomfortable, it doesn't hurt as bad as I thought.

I never imagined we'd be facing each other like this – with the lights on – but it makes it so much more intimate. I can see the tension in his jaw as he pushes forward again, feel the warmth of his breath as it quickens against my mouth. The fullness inside me is almost unbearable, but pleasurably so. I tighten my leg around his hip and he slides in deeper. Jase's eyes drift closed as a low guttural moan leaves his throat. 'Shit, baby, you're so tight.'

I think that must be a good thing by the effect it has on him. I almost giggle, but when Jase opens his eyes again, the intensity in them takes my breath away. 'You don't have to hold back…I like it.'

He groans again and kisses me deeply, his tongue gliding against mine as he thrusts into me hard. *Oh.* I didn't know it would feel like that. I pull a deep breath into my lungs as the last of my virginity is obliterated. Jase moves into me, his arms holding me tight against him and I'm lost to the sensations, the emotions flooding my system. Desire. Lust. Love. Things only Jase makes me feel.

His eyes meet mine, and he pushes the hair out of my face. 'Are you going to be able to come like this?'

It feels good, but I don't know. 'I'm not sure,' I answer honestly.

Jase reaches a hand between us, and just like he did up against the bathroom counter, he finds the spot that makes me tremble and massages it with the pad of his finger. Then he resumes thrusting into me, more slowly than before. I let my eyes slip close and focus on the sensations. Each time he thrusts in I whimper, and as he drags himself out slowly, I focus on the way he's caressing me. Soon I'm moaning out his name. Close…so close….

'Jassssse….' I come, loudly, my body shuddering against his.

Seconds later Jase groans and buries his face in my neck as he comes. His breath against my neck is the most erotic sound ever.

Afterwards, we lie together, a heap of warm heavy limbs and tangled sheets. Jase lightly strokes his fingertips against my arm. Everything about this moment is perfect.

'I love you, Whistle,' Jase whispers.

'I love you too.' Letting Jase in is scary, but I'm so glad I have. I feel him smile against my cheek. 'Was everything…okay?'

I lean up on my elbow to look down at him. Is he really asking me this? 'It was perfect.'

His grin is huge, and his eyes dance on mine. Okay, so he's clearly proud of his performance. His enthusiasm makes me smile. His thumb lightly strokes my cheek and his voice drops lower. 'So you'll be ready to go again then?'

'Is that a challenge?' I ask.

'Yes,' his voice is firm.

I shake my head. 'No. No more challenges.'

'Are you done with me now?' He chuckles.

My mouth turns up a notch. 'No. I'm just ready for you in a new way.' The future lies out wide and open in front of me. And I'm ready to live.

Wrapping his palm around the back of my neck, he guides my mouth to his.

Chapter 32

Avery

Entering the classroom for our Human Sexuality final, Jase begins chuckling. I turn to see what's caught his eye. *Self-Love 101* is written on the white board at the front of the room. Oh, this should be interesting. Professor Gibbs hadn't given us any indication what would be on the final today, and now suddenly I'm nervous.

Once the class is settled, Professor Gibbs sets my mind at ease. All we have to do is write one last journal assignment on what we've learned in his class, and we'll turn this in as our final.

We get to work, and Jase steals glances me throughout the hour-long class, a little smirk tugging his lips. I wonder how much of his paper is about me. I will kill him if he writes anything embarrassing. Especially anything about my first orgasm. I glance at his paper and swear I see the word *Whistle*. He clucks and shakes his head, shielding the page from my view. I narrow my eyes and keep writing.

Once our papers are turned in, Professor Gibbs invites anyone who cares to share to tell the class what they've learned. The old me would've hung my head, dare not make eye contact with him for fear of being called on. The new me has butterflies in her belly, half of me wanting to raise my hand, the other half nervous and unsure.

A girl in the back shouts out, 'Communication during sex is important. We've gotta teach guys what we like!'

The class erupts in laughter.

A guy sitting in front of me with a mop of blond curls raises his hand. 'Use lotion. Less chafing.'

I roll my eyes. A few more people speak up, and most of them take it seriously. The girl next to me says she's learned if you want a real relationship, not to jump into bed right away. Jase surprises me by raising his hand next. I'm more than a little curious about what's on his mind.

'I learned a lot this semester. I met this amazing girl, and we worked on her ability to...O...I mean *overcome* some fears and insecurities. And I learned it's more fun to give than to receive.'

My face goes bright red. I want to kick him. But when his gaze meets mine, I just smile at him. A big, dumb, I'm-totally-in-love-with-you grin. It's the same grin he's giving me. With Jase's encouragement, my butterflies take a leave of absence and I raise my hand.

'Avery,' Professor Gibbs nods.

'If something doesn't feel right, don't do it. And most importantly, *never* film it.'

Once the words leave my lips, I'm a little unsure if I should've said all that. It's probably too bold to put that out there, but hey, let them wonder. I have nothing to hide. Anymore.

'Amen sister,' a girl calls from the back of the room and my nerves ease.

Jase is watching me, his blue eyes dancing on mine. No regrets. Just life lessons. And I'm feeling pretty good about what I've learned.

The End

Acknowledgements

Thank you so very much to my lovely, sexy readers. I adore you guys! You make this journey so much fun, and I love connecting with you on Facebook and Twitter. Make sure you come say hiiiii!

A special thank you goes to my beta readers: Sali Powers and Miss Ellie. You are each so dear to me; thank you for all your support and advice. Thank you to my critique partners, and fellow new adult authors, Kylie Scott and Clare James. You each challenged me to improve and helped with the growth of these two characters and storyline. You gals are fab! A special thank you to my friends and writing group here in Minneapolis: Sara, Dawn, Kitty, Kari Marie, Liz, Nikki and our token male, Jonathan. There's no one else I'd rather get kicked out of the library with!

To Carmen Erickson, I'm so honored to work with you. Thank you for your thoughtful guidance on this manuscript. You rock, lady! In addition, Sara Biren at Stubby Pencil, holla girl. You're fantastic. Best. Editors. Ever. I feel so blessed!

I would also like to give a little shout out to the amazing bands that inspire my writing. I fueled up on plenty of The Xx, Lana Del Rey, Snow Patrol, The Bravery, and The Breezes while writing this. I hope you go give them a listen.

In addition, I must thank the dear Christine from Shh Mom's Reading for hosting my blog tour and arranging so many fun interviews, teasers and posts with over 30 blogs! Thank you for your support. And to the blogs who took the time to read and review my book, thank you so much for helping to spread the word. I heart book bloggers. Bookish girls rule!

My dear husband....I'm so lucky to be married to such a cute boy. Love you, 'Whistle.'